Golden Ticket

Kate Egan

FEIWEL AND FRIENDS
NEW YORK

A Feiwel and Friends Book
An imprint of Macmillan Publishing Group, LLC
120 Broadway, New York, NY 10271 • mackids.com

Our books may be purchased in bulk for promotional, educational, or business
use. Please contact your local bookseller or the Macmillan Corporate and
Premium Sales Department at (800) 221-7945 ext. 5442 or by email at
MacmillanSpecialMarkets@macmillan.com.

Library of Congress Cataloging-in-Publication Data

Names: Egan, Kate, author.
Title: Golden ticket / Kate Egan.
Description: First edition. | New York : Feiwel and Friends, 2022. |
    Audience: Ages 8–12. | Audience: Grades 4–6. | Summary: Eleven-year-old
    girl Ash McNulty struggles to keep up keep up with her fellow "Gifted
    and Talented" classmates, but when her plan to win the Quiz Bowl to show
    she is still on top backfires, she learns that there are many ways to be
    special.
Identifiers: LCCN 2021051193 | ISBN 9781250820334 (hardcover)
Subjects: CYAC: Gifted children—Fiction. | Self-esteem—Fiction. |
    Schools—Fiction.
Classification: LCC PZ7.E2773 Go 2022 | DDC [Fic]—dc23
LC record available at https://lccn.loc.gov/2021051193

First edition, 2022
Book design by Mallory Grigg
Feiwel and Friends logo designed by Filomena Tuosto
Printed in the United States of America by Sheridan, Brainerd,
Minnesota

ISBN 978-1-250-82033-4 (hardcover)
10 9 8 7 6 5 4 3 2 1

For Maddie,
who is not (and never has been) Ash McNulty,
and who has her own stories to tell

Chapter One

Every morning, while most kids zigzagged across town in yellow buses, Ash McNulty got to school on her own two feet. She could leave home just minutes before the bell and still arrive early, since she lived six houses away from the front entrance.

Today, though, Ash almost wished she weren't a walker. It was spring in other places, but winter was still holding on in her small town in Maine. From the fogged-up kitchen window, Ash saw an angry gray sky and a shower of frozen rain, more like slush really, pouring down on what was left of the snow in her family's front yard. April wasn't supposed to be like this.

Ash zipped her coat and put on her hood, pulling the drawstring so tight that only her eyes and nose were showing. Her younger sister, Gracie, clutched the only umbrella they could find between them.

"Ready?" Gracie said. Their parents had already left for a staff meeting at work, but the girls were old enough to get to school on their own now. Ash nodded, pulled open the door, and locked it as fast as she could.

Her hood was soaked and slipping over her eyes in two seconds flat, and by the time Ash wrenched it off, Gracie was halfway to school, using the umbrella like a shield to push her way through the sleet. Gracie waited at the school's front door as Ash peeled her coat open. Then she handed Ash the umbrella, leading the way inside and announcing, "You can have it for the walk home."

"Thanks," Ash replied. "But you should keep it— I'm staying after for Quiz Bowl practice, remember?"

Just saying the words was enough to make her nervous. The Quigley School Quiz Bowl was only three days away!

The Quiz Bowl was technically a fundraiser, but everyone knew it was way more than that. It was like a party and a contest all rolled into one. Teachers, parents, little brothers and sisters, even kids who'd finished Quigley years ago—everyone in town came out on a Friday night to feast at the cookie buffet and cheer on the brave kids who volunteered to answer trivia questions on stage. It was almost a given that a fifth grader would win—after all, the fifth graders were the oldest kids in school. Last year, though, there was a surprise upset, and a supersmart fourth grader—Ash herself!—had taken the top spot.

Now, of course, she had to do it all over again. She *had* to.

"Oh yeah," Gracie said, like the Quiz Bowl was just some distant memory. "Well, good luck with that. See you later!" She shrugged and headed away, twirling the umbrella.

Shaking her hair out, Ash headed down a quiet hallway in the direction of her classroom. She might be wet and freezing, but the steady hum of the copy machine and the smell of coffee from the teachers' room warmed her up. The school secretary, Ms. Caruso, waved from behind her window, and Ash sighed. If only the whole day would feel so calm and cozy.

Ms. Cooper, Ash's teacher, was stapling papers in her classroom upstairs. "What happened?" she asked. "You're drenched!" Ash hung up her dripping coat and stood next to the radiator until she got too hot. Then Ms. Cooper handed her the papers, and Ash got to work.

Since Ash was a walker and an early bird, she often helped Ms. Cooper get ready for the morning. This used to be her favorite part of the day, but now it was the part when the butterflies started swirling in her stomach. One of these days, her secret would be out. Would it be today? She tried not to think about it as she filled every student's mailbox.

Now Ash could hear her classmates in the hallway, barreling toward room 204 like a mob. When the door swung open, twenty people entered all at once, shedding winter gear. Soon the dirty snow would finally dissolve into muck, but right now that still seemed a long way off. As the other fifth graders removed their boots and put on their inside shoes, the classroom filled with the sound of zippers and the squelch of wet socks.

There was a lot on her mind, but some habits were automatic. Ash rushed to her desk to protect it before it was too late.

"Hey, Ash," Caden said as he dumped his backpack on the desk next to hers. A cloud of sand rose out of it and settled all over her stuff. He had a light orange ring around his lips, like he should have used a napkin after breakfast.

"Hi, Caden," Ash said tightly. She moved her pencil case into her desk so it wouldn't get crushed.

"Twinsies!" Ellie announced. She was still in the doorway, but her greeting was for Ash.

They were the furthest thing from twinsies. Ellie had long, shiny black hair, while Ash's was not even a recognizable color—a little red, a little brown—and not quite in a ponytail. The doctor said that Ellie was on track to be six feet tall, and Ash was still waiting for a growth spurt. But Ash called back "Twinsies!" because she and Ellie had the same lime-green parka.

Ellie hung hers up next to Ash's and eyed her desk, on the other side of Caden's. Ellie was Ash's ally in an ongoing battle. When Ash was out of the classroom, Ellie made sure Caden's mess didn't spread.

Before Morning Meeting, the other kids scrambled to check their mailboxes and sharpen their pencils and sign in for school lunch. Ash was ahead of everyone else, though, so she just waited. This happened to her a lot. She opened to chapter eight of a book she kept on hand for just this reason. She was with Lucy Pevensie, looking for Edmund in Narnia, when Ms. Cooper triple-clapped to get her class's attention.

"Welcome, friends," she said, "to a cheerful Tuesday morning." To Ms. Cooper, *every* morning was cheerful.

She began the day with some important business: Permission slips were due soon for the fifth-grade trip to Funtown. Ash still remembered when she was back in kindergarten, counting how long it would be before she was old enough for this field trip to the amusement park. Finally it was going be her turn! The class did a few stretches and listened to more announcements.

"Now that we've exercised our bodies," Ms. Cooper said, "let's begin to exercise our minds!" First up was the Word of the Day—a vocabulary challenge. "Does anyone know what this one means?" Ms. Cooper asked.

It was a short word—*g-a-r-b*—but Ash didn't know it.

I should know it, Ash thought. People would expect her to know it.

Her mind raced. Did it have to do with trash? Like garbage?

Or maybe it was like *grab*—switch two letters, and the two words were the same.

Or what if it was something to eat? Now Ash was wildly guessing.

Caden leaned over until his elbow was almost in her belly button. "Well?" he whispered. Caden thought she was a walking dictionary. He was sure that, if anyone knew what *garb* was, it was Ash.

That was because Ash was sort of in Ms. Cooper's class, but also sort of in another one. She'd hear all about Ms. Cooper's plans for the day, but she wouldn't actually take part in them since the minute that language arts time started, Ash would leave this classroom and go downstairs. She was in Mr. Lopez's class for language arts and math, ninety minutes for each subject. By the time you added in lunch and recess, plus specials like gym and art, Ash was out of Ms. Cooper's room more than she was in it. Her most-of-the-time teacher was actually Mr. Lopez.

Ash's other class was called Talent Development. People called it GT, though, for gifted and talented, and you carried the label from the minute you got a high score on one test in second grade. The top 2 percent of the school went to Mr. Lopez, and Ash had been going for so long that GT was like a part of her name by now.

G-a-r-b. For some reason, the word reminded Ash of Halloween. She raised her hand and waited to be called on. No one else was even trying.

"Ash?" said Ms. Cooper.

"Is it like . . . a costume?" she guessed.

The teacher's smile was a ray of sunshine. "Yes, it can

be," she replied. "Garb is any kind of special clothing. Like a uniform, or a ball gown. Even a wizard's robes."

Hands shot up as people offered other examples. Motorcycle jackets. Bowling shoes. Tutus.

Caden jabbed Ash in the ribs. "You're twelve for twelve," he announced. She shrugged modestly, but she had been keeping careful track of her record, too. A run like this was what she'd need in the Quiz Bowl. Ellie gave her a thumbs-up and an eye roll at the same time. Thumbs-up for the right answer, eye roll for Caden.

Then Ms. Cooper's phone started jumping around on her desk. The ringer was off, but it was vibrating like crazy. She glanced down, and she must have seen that the call was from someone inside the school, because she held her finger up. That was her sign for the class to keep quiet and wait. Ash was about to return to Narnia when she heard her name.

"Ash McNulty?" said Ms. Cooper into the silence. "Of course. I'll send her right down." She ended the call and told Ash, "They want to see you in the office, sweetie."

Oh no, Ash thought. *This is it.*

She stood up stiffly, as if she had just stepped out of a freezer.

"Ooooh, you're in trouble!" someone called out, and everyone else laughed. Ash was the last kid anyone expected to get in trouble.

When Ms. Cooper gave her the hall pass, Ash acted like everything was normal, but she was about to crack. Her parents were going to be in the office, she just knew it. That's what happened when things were serious—they brought in your parents without telling you. An ambush. Soon everyone would know she was a fake. A girl with a disappointing report card stuffed in the back of her closet. A GT kid who was quietly falling behind.

Her eyes welled up as she walked robotically down the hall and toward the stairs. Ash went this way so often that she could do it blindfolded. Mr. Lopez's classroom was on the first floor, right next to the office. *What if I run into him?* Ash thought, panicked. Then she realized he would probably be in the meeting, too.

Ash made a quick stop in the bathroom and ran some ice-cold water onto a paper towel. She scrunched it up and pressed the ball to her eyes, shocking her tears before they started to flow, then scurried out of the bathroom and into the stairwell. No one was there, thankfully. Every teacher and every student was in Morning Meeting—that was the routine at Marion Quigley Elementary.

But no—there was a parent on the loose. Here was Mrs. Silver, marching upstairs importantly with a towering stack of folders. She was the president of the parents' group, a volunteer extraordinaire. Ash's mom was not her biggest fan. "She's a busybody, Ash," her mom said. "Always listening. Don't say anything to Elena Silver unless you want it repeated all over town." She would wonder where Ash was going, for sure.

From her enthusiastic greeting, you might think she was Ash's best friend. "Well, hello there," Mrs. Silver said so loudly that her voice rattled the artwork on the walls. "You're getting so grown up. Off to junior high in the fall, right?" She paused as Ash nodded, then moved to the kicker. "Or are you taking classes at the high school yet?"

It was kind of a sore subject that her son, Sammy Silver, was not in the Talent Development class. Every year, his mom had him privately retested just to see if he could score high enough to qualify, but apparently he never made it. As far as Ash could tell, Sammy Silver's favorite subject was recess.

One day last year, Ash had overheard Mrs. Silver on the playground, speaking to someone's dad in a fierce tone. It took Ash a second to realize she was talking about the GT program.

"It's practically like a private school," Mrs. Silver said bitterly. "The best teacher, for such a tiny group of students. Who wouldn't succeed in a class like that?" She took off her sunglasses to glare at the dad. "Those kids get picked out when they're seven years old, and they get handed a golden ticket. Of course they become stars. We reap what we sow." Sammy's mom shook her head, as if her son would never sprout. Always the silver, never the gold.

Mrs. Silver had chaperoned every field trip Ash could remember since preschool. She had clipped a million coupons for Quigley and even DJed the school dance. In spite of what her mom said, Ash thought she was nice. But she wished Mrs. Silver would stop pretending Ash could skip four grades.

Ash shook her head. "No high school for me, Mrs. Silver," she said. "Not yet." She wondered how she would escape. Being trapped in the stairwell was almost as bad as going to the office.

Luckily, her good reputation saved her. "Delivering the attendance sheet?" Mrs. Silver guessed. "I won't keep you. Ms. Cooper is counting on your help!" She stepped out of the way and let Ash pass.

Attendance was automated these days, so no one had delivered an attendance sheet to the office since last century, but Mrs. Silver didn't need to know that. She didn't need to know that Ash had been called to the principal, or why. Ash waved miserably and headed for her doom.

Somehow she arrived at the office. She slipped past

a line of tardy kids at the secretary's desk and walked beyond it, to where everyone would be waiting. The door to the principal's office was wide open, but she didn't see Mr. Lopez or her parents. For a moment she wondered if they were hiding, like at a surprise party, ready to spring out as soon as she walked in. But the only surprise happened when the principal, Mrs. Shepard, arrived with a girl who'd been swallowed by a big gray sweatshirt.

Mrs. Shepard smiled warmly and introduced Ash to the girl. "Please welcome Tilly, our newest fifth grader. Just last week, she moved all the way from Florida. I'm assigning you to be her guide, Ash. I know you'll do a great job of showing her the ropes at Quigley." She went on to explain that Ash was someone really special, a leader and a role model, and that Ash would show Tilly everything she needed to succeed.

Ash probably looked embarrassed, but mainly she was relieved.

It was not an intervention. It was not a conference.

Her parents were still at work, and Mr. Lopez was getting ready for language arts, which would be starting any minute. She hadn't been found out. In fact, she'd been chosen. She was the handpicked tour guide for this scrawny girl. She was still golden for now.

Chapter Two

Tilly watched Ash curiously as they walked down the hall. "Are you okay?" she asked. "Your eyes are all red."

"Allergies," Ash said.

"This time of year?" Tilly asked. She didn't miss a beat.

Someone must have filled her in on the patterns of Maine's four seasons, because Ash was pretty sure there was only one season in Florida.

"Or maybe I'm getting sick," Ash said quickly. "Anyway, welcome to Quigley."

She was keenly aware that Mrs. Shepard was just steps ahead of them. Some kids were in the hallway, now that Morning Meeting was over. When Mrs. Shepard stepped toward them, they scattered like confetti. She was a big person, like a basketball player, in a bright red blazer and a heavy silver necklace. People liked Mrs. Shepard, but no one ever got too close.

She stopped a third grader to ask about his dad, who was in the hospital. Then a teacher grabbed her arm and started talking. Meanwhile, Ash and Tilly just kind of stood there. *What am I supposed to do now?* Ash wondered. What would a fifth-grade leader do, if she still was one? Would she go into tour-guide mode? Ash cared more about making a good impression on Mrs. Shepard than about making a good impression on Tilly. She'd start to show the new girl around, Ash decided, and Mrs. Shepard could catch up when she was ready.

She motioned for Tilly to follow her. "So . . . ," Ash said. "The younger kids have this whole floor to themselves. Third, fourth, and fifth graders are upstairs." They passed a long line of classrooms on their way to the art and music rooms. Ash showed her the gym—echoing and empty at this time of day, its floors shining like a mirror—and the cafeteria, which was still serving breakfast to go. Ash showed her the spacious bathrooms and the volunteer room, where Mrs. Silver was making copies. There was a bright nook, halfway down the hall, where groups of kids could gather to work together. There were smaller rooms between the classrooms, for the same purpose. "That way if you need extra help," Ash explained, "there's someplace for you to work one-on-one with an adult." For all she knew, Tilly needed extra help all the time.

It was funny to see Quigley through Tilly's eyes. It was a regular public school, but it was built only a few years ago, so it was still really nice—it even had that new-school smell of fresh paint and raw wood. Ash's parents complained about the parking for school events, and some kids felt lost in such a big building, but Ash didn't think Tilly was noticing any of these problems. Her eyes widened as the tour continued. A strand of yellow hair peeked out from under her hood, but most of her face was still hidden in the sweatshirt. Ash couldn't even see her fingers.

They walked into the art room, where watercolors

had been left on a shelf to dry. Ash introduced Tilly to Mr. Bones, the skeleton that stood by the door, wearing a beret and holding a painter's palette. At last, Tilly spoke. "This art room is huge," she said. "Nothing like my old school." Ash didn't ask about her old school, because she was too eager to show that Quigley had a kiln for baking pottery. Tilly actually smiled. Her front teeth overlapped a little, and Ash wondered if that meant she needed braces. Kids in their grade were starting to get them now.

The music room was right next door, a tangle of black music stands. "Fifth graders can play an instrument," Ash told her. "We have band twice a week, and there's a concert in June." She remembered this because it was always on her birthday.

Tilly started to emerge from her sweatshirt, like a turtle coming out of its shell. Her neck stretched, and she swept the hood off to reveal a blond mop. "You think I can join in the middle of the year?" she asked. "I'd love to play the clarinet."

Ash didn't know. They'd been working on their

songs since September. Would Tilly be able to catch up? Being a new kid meant being out of step with the rhythm of the school, like when the drums came in at the wrong time on a song. It was going to take some time and practice before she got in sync with everyone else.

Ash was wondering if she should show her the playground when Mrs. Shepard appeared again. "I'm sorry, girls," she said. "Never a dull moment. Thank you for taking matters into your own hands." She turned to Tilly and said, "It's better to see Quigley through a student's eyes, anyway." Mrs. Shepard grinned. "Ash is one of our very best."

Ash wished she wouldn't say that.

And maybe it was her imagination, but Tilly's posture seemed to change, like she just remembered Ash had the flu and she didn't want to catch it.

"Why don't we head for your classroom?" Mrs. Shepard said to Tilly. "Get you settled in before . . . language arts? That's what fifth grade has first, Ash, correct?"

She nodded. "Who's your teacher, Tilly?" Ash asked, to signal that she was still friendly.

"Ms. Cooper," Tilly said.

Ash beamed. "I have her, too!" she said with pretend enthusiasm. Inside, she was cringing. Ash was the only person Tilly knew in the whole school, and she would be leaving as soon as they got back to their classroom, because Mr. Lopez was expecting her.

Tilly and Ash followed Mrs. Shepard upstairs and all the way back to Ms. Cooper's room. Mrs. Shepard took over the tour now, telling Tilly the kinds of things she might tell to adults. Stuff about student-teacher ratios, and after-school programs, and the coming transition to junior high. "As I was telling your mother . . . ," Mrs. Shepard said. Ash wondered where she was.

"We don't teach to the test here, of course," Mrs. Shepard promised. "But we use standardized test scores to make sure that all the students are challenged appropriately. Children who need extra help meeting the goals will have assistance. And children who have surpassed the goals will have accelerated work."

Tilly didn't ask any questions, but Ash wondered if she understood this lingo. She also wondered if Tilly's family picked this town because of its nice school. That was the whole idea when it was built, Ash knew. This town didn't have the most jobs or the biggest houses, but it had one of the best schools around. That was why her family lived here, for sure.

"Here we are!" said Mrs. Shepard. She knocked briskly on Ms. Cooper's door, and Ash led the way in. Caden was sharpening a pencil over her desk, and the shavings were in a filthy heap on her chair. Ash squinted at him: gotcha! He shrugged as if the pencil were out of his control.

For Tilly's sake, Ash hoped her desk would be far away from his. To her horror, Ms. Cooper had another plan.

She turned away from the board, where she'd been writing. "We are so happy to meet you, Tilly," Ms. Cooper said. "I think you'll feel right at home in our room. There's only one problem . . ."

Somehow, although Ms. Cooper had all Tilly's

records from her old school, a thick file full of information, she had not been able to get anyone to bring in an extra desk. "We will get that resolved today," Ms. Cooper promised her new student. "For the time being, though, you can sit in Ash's place. I see you two already know each other."

Caden swept the shavings away, and his fingers turned black. Now there were pencil streaks on the chair and a little pile of sawdust on the floor beneath it. Tilly looked confused. Why did she get the desk that was trashed? "But where is Ash going to sit?" she asked.

Caden explained, "Ash is going to her other class, where the smart kids are. You won't see her for a while."

So now Tilly had a dirty desk to sit at, in a room full of strangers, and a sudden understanding. This school had lots of bells and whistles, but not all of them were for her. She shrank back into her hood. Ash hated that moment, when other people saw that she had something they might like to have.

Too bad Tilly didn't know the whole story.

Ash fled before the new girl was fully settled, but by

the time she got to language arts, she was late. There was no sneaking past the GT kids: Five heads turned as soon as Ash opened the door.

"Sorry . . . ," she said. "Mrs. Shepard asked me to give someone a tour."

Ash's best friend, Jane, raised an eyebrow high enough to clear the frame of her red glasses. Her mother might be a lawyer, but Ash thought Jane could probably be a detective when she grew up. She knew Jane would want to know every detail: who needed the tour and why.

Mr. Lopez nodded, his shaved head catching the light. "Glad you could join us," he said.

Tilly would have been surprised if she'd seen this room. Rumor had it there had been a mistake during construction of the new school, and one classroom never got built. Instead, the builders put up a wall to divide a room they'd already made, creating two tiny spaces. Mr. Lopez had one, and the school nurse had the other, which meant that sometimes his class heard people throwing up next door.

It was a little crowded in Mr. Lopez's room, but no one was complaining. Instead of a tile floor, there was a bright rug that was supposed to absorb sound. Instead of desks, the kids all sat around a big table. Mr. Lopez was at the head, with a stack of papers where a plate would be if they were having a meal.

"We were just reviewing our figures of speech," he told Ash. "Remember, they help us spice up our writing." The rest of the fifth grade was still on nouns and verbs, as far as she knew.

Ash relaxed. She loved reviews.

Mr. Lopez said the figures of speech, and everyone gave examples in a quick call-and-response.

"Alliteration?" he ventured. That was the easiest one. Matching sounds at the beginning of every word.

"The big bad bear bounced," said Lane.

Mr. Lopez nodded and moved on. "Assonance?"

It was Sebastian's turn. "Sweet cream. Space age." He explained why these words were good examples. "They don't rhyme, and the spelling isn't the same. But the vowel sounds repeat."

"Onomatopoeia?" These were words that sounded like what they were describing—they were everybody's favorite.

"Whoosh!" Olivia called out.

"Splat," said Jane.

"Mooooooo," added Lane. He made a convincing cow, and they all laughed. Even a class of five could have a clown.

Ash's turn came on oxymoron. In her other class, you could bet a billion dollars that someone would make fun of the word. Someone who couldn't get past the *moron*. No one commented on it here.

"Oxymorons are two words that seem to contradict each other," she said. "Like old news, for instance. Open secret. Pretty ugly."

Mr. Lopez smiled. He was happy so far. "Okay, guys," he said. "I think we've got the hang of these. How about we see what they look like in their natural habitat?"

He waited expectantly. The moment lasted long enough for Ash to worry if she'd missed something

again. She opened her folder just as Sebastian's hand shot into the air. "Yes?" said Mr. Lopez.

"Metaphor!" Sebastian said triumphantly. "'Natural habitat' is a metaphor. Mr. Lopez is comparing words to plants or animals."

Ash met Jane's glance. *Know-it-all,* her eyes said. A little admiring, a little jealous.

Sebastian always seemed to be a step ahead.

And these days Ash was always a step behind.

She kept her eyes on her folder and her hands very still. She knew where this lesson was going.

A metaphor was a figure of speech, like its cousin the simile. In similes, the writer used the word *like* or *as,* which made them easy to spot. "As cold as ice" was a simile. So was "In like a lion, out like a lamb." But a metaphor was a comparison without any warning.

When Mr. Lopez talked about words in their natural habitat, Ash knew what he meant—words in a real piece of writing—without ever noticing that he was using a metaphor. Unless you were really paying attention, metaphors would sneak up on you like that. Ash could tell you what they were, no problem. But finding them by herself was like finding a needle in a haystack. Even though that phrase was a cliché.

Mr. Lopez peeled sheets off his stack of paper and handed them around. Each student had a different poem to read, he explained, and each poem contained many figures of speech, particularly metaphors. Today's work was to find as many as they could.

Ash frowned, and Mr. Lopez noticed. "Soon we will be writing poems of our own," he added, like that would be a treat. Ash wasn't thrilled about that, either. She was better at things that had answers.

Then a little bit of good luck came her way. Mr. Lopez wanted his students to work alone for a while. At least Ash wouldn't have to partner with Jane or Sebastian. No one would see her floundering.

Ash was at the foot of the table, with Lane on one side and Olivia on the other. She kept her eyes on her poem, scanning for alliteration or anything else, but she was distracted by the sound of their pencils, so smooth and so sure of themselves.

This metaphor hunt is like Animal Farm *all over again,* Ash thought.

Before they started reading it, Ash had thought that *Animal Farm* might be a book for preschoolers, with tabs that lifted up to show baby goats and friendly mice. Turned out it was a book for high schoolers, only Mr. Lopez was teaching it in fifth grade. And somehow Ash had missed the most important thing about it: The whole book was a metaphor.

What she'd thought was a story about two pigs making mischief in the barn—a little bit *Charlotte's Web*, a little bit *Click, Clack, Moo*—was actually a story about the leaders of a real country called the Soviet Union. Which didn't even exist anymore.

Mr. Lopez explained that the pigs Snowball and Napoleon were modeled after Soviet leaders named Trotsky and Stalin. They started out with grand plans for building a new government there, but it ended up worse than the government it replaced.

"Trotsky?" Lane asked. "Why didn't the author make him a horse?" Ash laughed along with the other kids, but that wasn't the only thing she didn't understand. *If the author had wanted to write about Trotsky and Stalin, why did he write about animals?* she wondered. And couldn't they just enjoy the story about the pigs without getting into politics?

Mr. Lopez gave the class a long list of new words and a crash course in history to go with *Animal Farm*. It was easy to memorize the words and the important dates, but Ash ran into trouble when she had to write an essay. Getting her first low grade—a Needs Improvement—was hard enough. But then she saw what Mr. Lopez wrote in his weekly report to Ms. Cooper: "Ash is having trouble with the abstract thinking required in our novel unit." That was when Ash realized she had a problem.

Because, if she was honest, the *Animal Farm* essay wasn't the only assignment she'd struggled with.

The geometry unit had been fine . . . until they got to theorems. Which were basically sentences, and Ash wasn't sure why they were part of math class. She still didn't know how or when to use them. And one of these days she had to get serious about the Island Project.

It was only a matter of time before Ash would have to talk to someone about her progress—or lack of progress—in Mr. Lopez's room. It was only a matter of time before she would have to get her report card, currently under a pile of stuffed animals, signed by a parent and returned to school. And, okay—the report card wasn't *that* bad. But it was way below Ash's usual standard, and that was bad enough. Maybe there would never be a meeting in the principal's office, but Ash wasn't sure. Did anyone know what happened when talent failed to develop?

Mrs. Shepard had told Tilly she was a fifth-grade leader. Caden thought she was a genius. Only Ash knew the truth: She was on the verge of trouble.

She was bad at abstract thinking—and she didn't even know what that was.

She was losing confidence day by day.

She was the slowest kid in the GT class, and getting slower.

If she couldn't keep up now, she might not be able to keep up when she went to junior high.

She might not be in the GT class at all.

And then where would she be?

No one would be handpicking her to give tours, or to help make a new kid feel at home, if that happened. No one would be saying she was the best. She'd be just like everyone else—and, even worse, the whole world would know what she'd lost. What would Mrs. Silver say? she wondered. Something like, *All that special treatment, wasted.* A little fake sympathy, then an all-out campaign to move Sammy into her spot at the top.

Quigley Elementary had experts who would help you catch up in math and reading. It had a speech therapist and a behavioral specialist. There were two guidance counselors and, as Mrs. Shepard would tell you, a top-notch group of teachers. But no one at Quigley could fix Ash's problem. The minute she asked for help, they'd know she wasn't gifted. She'd be out of the program before she could prove that she still belonged.

Luckily, Ash had a plan.

This Friday, she hoped, the Quiz Bowl was going to fix everything. For the second year in a row, she'd take home the grand prize!

More importantly, though, she'd send a message with every right answer in the Quiz Bowl. She was still smart, and she was still special.

After her triumph, her parents would be a little less likely to use words like *let down* when they saw the report card.

After her triumph, Ash could stop making excuses, regain her pride, and somehow get herself back on track.

Ash looked up from her poem. Sitting around the table, the other kids looked almost like they were eating dinner at home. She'd known them for so long they were like brothers and sisters. *You need to get it together*, she told herself. *You can't be the black sheep of this family.*

She had just noticed that *black sheep* was a metaphor when she heard Mr. Lopez beside her. He said, "Ash, can you step outside to talk?"

Chapter Three

The Talent Development room didn't have any extra space, so Mr. Lopez liked to have important conversations in the hallway. Sometimes he wanted to know if the homework load was too heavy or help iron out problems between kids in the class. There was nothing unusual about Mr. Lopez closing the door behind them, but Ash wished that someone would come down the hallway with, say, a motorcycle. Something loud enough to drown out the sound of her beating heart. What did they need to discuss?

Mr. Lopez adjusted his tie. He *always* wore a tie. "I just wanted to touch base with you, Ash," he said. "Everything good?"

"Um . . . yeah . . ." Ash stammered, staring at the floor.

Mr. Lopez seemed nervous, too. He rubbed his bald

head like a magic lamp, then said, "Look, I know you weren't happy when I returned the *Animal Farm* essays. I was thinking it over later—pondering, you might say—and then I had an epiphany. That is, a great idea."

Ash could still remember how she felt when she saw that *Needs Improvement*. Just like the essay, Ash *herself* needed improvement, she'd realized. Why hadn't she seen it before?

"I thought you might like to do a rewrite," Mr. Lopez continued. "Give it another try. With the feedback I gave you, I know you can get it into better shape. Spruce it up, right?"

Kids in Ms. Cooper's class did rewrites all the time, but Mr. Lopez never offered that option. *His* students got things right the first time around, Ash thought.

"Oh," she said, blinking. "Thanks! I mean ... I'm not sure what to say ..."

She really just wanted to forget the essay had ever happened. Once she won the Quiz Bowl, would it even matter?

"You'll have a road map if you read my comments,"

Mr. Lopez said. "Or we can do some brainstorming together. Whatever it takes. I just want to see you grasp the ideas, you know?" He pretended to grasp an idea out of the air.

Mr. Lopez paused to let Ash speak, then covered over her silence with more words. "You can think it over. But it might be helpful. Everyone needs a second chance sometimes."

"Speaking of second chances . . . or maybe third . . . ," Ash said, changing the subject abruptly, "I can't believe I forgot my report card again. I'll bring it in tomorrow, okay?"

She hated the feeling of telling this lie. When Caden forgot to bring in his signed report card for Ms. Cooper, he'd had to have an inside recess, but GT kids got a little extra leeway like that. She had to bluff only a little longer now. Once the Quiz Bowl was over, she could hold her head high.

Mr. Lopez had no reason not to believe her. "I know, I know," he said, waving it off. "Don't worry about it. Just get it to me when you can."

Now Ash did some quick calculations in her head. The *Needs Improvement* had been folded into the B minus she got on her report card. Rewriting wouldn't get her back on the honor roll. But she could stay on Mr. Lopez's good side . . .

"Can I get back to you on the rewrite?" Ash asked.

"Great!" said Mr. Lopez. "Just know I'm here for you. Truly. I want to see you do your best work, Ash." He high-fived her and opened the door to the classroom again. It was silent except for the sound of someone blowing their nose on the nurse's side of the wall.

His offer stayed in the back of Ash's mind as she finished reading her poem. Was it okay to take a second chance? she wondered. She could never erase the mistakes she'd made the first time—Mr. Lopez would always know what she didn't know. Teachers were always saying that students needed a "growth mindset," that they needed to accept they wouldn't get everything on the first try. That was all okay, Ash thought, but why did it seem like she was the only GT student who needed a redo? Sebastian got extra coaching for social skills, but he got answers—and digested ideas—faster than a computer.

Most days, Ash went back to Ms. Cooper's room when language arts was over, but today Mr. Lopez kept his crew for some extra planning, since they were starting to make decisions about their Island Projects. The Island Project was another fifth-grade rite of passage, like the trip to Funtown. It had been a Quigley tradition before Quigley was even in this new building, and the GT kids were taking part just like everybody else.

The Island Project was supposed to teach fifth graders how to break down a long-term assignment before they got to the big time: junior high. The basic assignment was to design an imaginary island that showed off certain geography concepts. Every island needed a theme, and certain elements like latitude and longitude were required, but otherwise the students had a lot of freedom. Some people were doing maps of their islands, some were doing 3D models, and some were still figuring it out.

Ellie was doing Ice Cream Island, Ash knew, and

Caden was doing Fortnite Island. As for her own project? Well, at this point Ash wasn't even sure what she was doing. She and Jane usually teamed up for things if they could, but Jane had a way of taking over. And who was Ash to question her right now?

"So I found the best website last night," Jane told Ash, motioning to the seat next to her and opening a laptop. "Check out these pictures!"

Ash squinted to see tiny pinpricks of light on the laptop's dark screen.

"They're moons!" Jane exclaimed. She zoomed in on one of them so Ash could see its colors and patterns, plus their swirling reflection in Jane's glasses. The sight made Ash feel unsettled.

Jane was the sort of person who got obsessed with one thing and thought about only that thing until she moved on to something else. Last year it was dystopian novels, and the year before that it was knitting. Now it was space, and if Ash wanted Jane as a partner, she would have to go along with it. The way she always had to go along with Jane as her friend.

Just then, Jane made her announcement. "So I'm thinking we'll do Moon Island," she said, "featuring all the moons of the solar system. Did you know that Saturn might have up to eighty-two of them?"

Back when she was younger, Ash had dreamed of doing an island that would draw crowds at Island Night, when all the parents came to see the fifth graders' work, but now that seemed a little risky. What if she aimed for something awesome, all on her own, and it fell flat? Ash couldn't afford that right now. Jane's moons were safer, for sure.

"Cool!" she said. That was all she could manage.

"Great!" said Jane, and the decision was made. "So, Mercury and Venus don't have any moons, but Earth has one, of course, and Mars has two . . ."

Politely, Ash swallowed a yawn. Her mind drifted to black holes and deep space, way more mysterious and fascinating. Jane opened several tabs on the laptop and started a page of notes. "How about you watch this video?" she suggested. Or maybe ordered.

Ash was relieved when it was time for art with Ms.

Cooper's class. Then—finally!—lunch! The morning was over.

Now that their parents left for work so early, she and Gracie were supposed to make their own break-fast. Ash had skipped it today, though, and her stomach was growling. She was at the head of the line as Ms. Cooper's class made its way downstairs.

The cafeteria was filled with bright light and the dull roar of the fifth grade before feeding time. Some kids were tearing into lunches they'd brought from home, while Ash grabbed a tray and headed for the hot-lunch line, scanning the room for Jane. Somehow Ellie got ahead of her, waving a chocolate-milk carton in the air. "Ash!" she called out. "We'll be in the corner."

Sometimes Ash sat with Ellie, but today she had a "working lunch," as Jane called it, which was really some last-minute cramming for the Quiz Bowl. It took Ash a second to realize that "we" was Ellie and the new girl, Tilly. She was still in her XL sweatshirt and hold-ing up the line as she learned the routine. "Hurry up!" someone grumbled. "We don't have all day!"

Ellie and Tilly were settling at their table by the time Ash had her turkey burger. Ash stopped to say hi, and Tilly caught Ash's eye as she unwrapped a grilled cheese. Tilly nodded, but she didn't smile. Ash could hardly blame her. The first day in a new school couldn't be much fun. She hoped Tilly had a new desk, at least.

Ellie was telling Tilly everything she needed to know about the cafeteria. "Eating is the easy part," she explained. "But when you throw away the trash, there are like six different buckets for different kinds of recycling. Better not mix them up, or you'll be in big trouble."

"What kind of trouble?" Tilly asked.

"Nothing too bad," Ash reassured the new girl. "You might have to wipe down the tables or something."

Tilly scooted over to make room for Ash just as Jane, at the next table, pointed to her smartwatch.

"Oh, no, that's okay," Ash told Tilly. "My friend Jane is actually waiting for me. We have to . . . go over something." Ash wasn't sure why it was so hard to explain that they were going to test each other with trivia questions. It seemed a little too serious and also a little too . . . trivial.

Tilly did that thing again, where she kind of shrank down into a smaller size. Her voice was hard when she said, "Oh, I forgot. You're too good for the rest of us."

Maybe people thought that, but no one actually said that to Ash, ever. People just treated her like she was important. Now she could feel her ears burning red and her grip on the lunch tray shaking as she turned around. She could also feel Tilly's gaze burning into her back. Ash hoped that Ellie would change the subject quickly.

"What took so long?" Jane asked as soon as Ash's tray hit the table. "It's grind time!"

"Sorry!" Ash said. She dropped her voice to a whisper, adding, "That's the new girl I gave the tour to." She didn't dare to look, but she shook her head in the right direction.

Jane took a quick peek at Tilly and said, "Her sweatshirt is bigger than she is!" But Jane was laser-focused on the Quiz Bowl, so she didn't dwell on Tilly for long. "I think we should practice the geography questions.

We're pretty good on the other categories, don't you think?"

Ash took a bite of her burger as Jane popped the first question. She didn't know the answer, but at least it blocked out what Tilly had said. Ash didn't think she was too good for anyone. If anything, she thought she wasn't good enough!

"What country has the world's longest coastline?" Jane asked.

"Um . . . Australia," Ash guessed.

"Nope," said Jane. "Canada."

She flipped another card over. "What's the capital of Chile?"

"Caracas!" said Ash. "Oh, wait . . . no . . . that might be Venezuela . . ."

"Santiago," Jane replied.

Ash tried not to panic. Two wrong in a row. If this happened Friday night, she'd be out of the Quiz Bowl.

At least it was her turn to ask now, and she was pretty sure Jane wouldn't know this one. "What's the largest desert in the world?" she said.

Jane didn't miss a beat. "Antarctica," she replied.

For the hundredth time, Ash wished that Jane wasn't her chief competition at the Quiz Bowl.

The next question flew at Ash before she could finish that thought. "Okay . . . how many US states are landlocked?" asked Jane.

Ash was trying to imagine the map and count the states in her mind, when Tilly piped up from behind them.

"Knowing all that stuff doesn't make you smart," she announced. "Even a robot could memorize all those answers. Robots can win against people at poker, you know."

Jane hadn't even met Tilly yet! Ash bristled on her friend's behalf. But Jane just offered up what Ash knew was a fake smile, along with a fake invitation.

"We're getting ready for the Quiz Bowl on Friday night," Jane said coolly. "It's not too late for you to sign up!" She didn't say the rest of her sentence out loud, but she didn't need to: *Then we'll see who's really smart here.*

As if Ash wasn't nervous enough already.

"Let's move on to the pop-culture questions," Jane said. It was as if they had never been interrupted. Jane's lunch was untouched, but she had an endless appetite for trivia. "Your turn."

Ash moved on to the next category. "Okay," she said. "Who starred in the 2012 film *Pitch Perfect*?" Jane paused, and Ash took a deep breath. At least she knew *that* one.

Her eyes wandered back to Tilly. *I'll show her*, Ash thought.

Soon the first bell rang, and the first wave of kids washed toward the six categories of trash. Sure enough, Tilly put a glass bottle in a bucket clearly marked PLAS-TIC. Jane saw it, too, and commented as they headed out for recess. "Doesn't seem like the sharpest crayon in the box, does she?" It sounded like something Jane's mom would say. For a second, Ash felt almost sorry for the new girl.

As usual, Ash and Jane spent recess on top of the Pyramid, a huge climbing structure on Quigley's playground. They did a few flips on the bars, and Ash hung upside down for a while, but mostly they continued to quiz each other while the rest of the fifth grade ran wild. In many ways, Ash and Jane were above it all. When the bell rang they scattered in different directions, as they had to line up with their separate classes, and Ash called out, "See you after school!"

That was definitely the plan. But by the end of the day, Ash was right in the middle of a project with Ms. Cooper's class. They had gathered in the gym to paint a banner for the Quiz Bowl, and Ash didn't know how to leave without being rude. "Friday is gonna be your night!" Caden kept saying, and Ash really wished there was a way Caden could make that happen. In the meantime, she had to protect the art supplies from him at all costs. He was not a kid you could trust around glitter.

Ash outlined each letter on the banner with marker; then Ellie filled it in with paint. Ms. Cooper added some sparkle, and the two girls dabbed the glitter up carefully so it didn't spread across the gym. Then Tilly—of all people—drew the school mascot beneath the letters. Ash had to admit it looked exactly like a real snowy owl, with bright eyes and speckled feathers. Even Caden noticed. "Have you ever drawn an owl before?" he demanded to know. "Was it also the mascot at your old school? Or are you just a great artist?" Tilly shrugged and gave him a shy, snaggletoothed smile.

While the banner dried, Ms. Cooper let her kids play a little freeze tag, and soon the gym was filled with the squeak of sneakers on the shiny floor. When Ash got tagged, she stood under the basketball net, catching her breath and waving frantically for Ellie to free her. By now, Ash knew, Jane would be in Mr. Lopez's room, watching old episodes of *Jeopardy!* with Lane and shouting out the answers, but Ash didn't feel like joining them quite yet. Most of her classmates had stayed for the late bus, and she wanted to be there to hang the banner above the stage. Plus . . . freeze tag was super fun!

Ms. Cooper stood on a ladder holding one end of the banner, and Ellie was waiting with the other side, when Ms. Cooper realized she'd left her masking tape upstairs. Once again, Ash was chosen. "Would you mind running upstairs to get it?" her teacher asked. "It's right in my top desk drawer."

Ash tiptoed past Mr. Lopez's room and sprinted to Ms. Cooper's, feeling freer than she'd felt all day. Inside the classroom, Ash inspected her desk. Thankfully, there was no sign of Caden's pencil shavings. There was a new desk in the hallway, actually—it had to be for Tilly—and the folder from Tilly's old school was still on top of Ms. Cooper's desk.

Ash gulped before she opened the drawer. It was a big deal to go into a teacher's desk, even for her. Ash felt proud that teachers thought she was trustworthy as well as smart.

But her honesty was put to the test as soon as she reached for the masking tape. Because beneath the tape there was another folder, and this one was clearly labeled.

The label said: CONFIDENTIAL. FIFTH-GRADE QUIZ BOWL QUESTIONS/ANSWERS.

Chapter Four

Ash snapped into action. For once in her life, she didn't even think.

She knew that what she was about to do was not okay, but she also knew that she was going to do it. No question about it. She had to.

Most fifth graders didn't have phones, and most people didn't know that she did. Ash's phone was an ancient model with a feeble battery, and Ash barely used it, just moved it out of yesterday's pocket every morning. But now that her parents were so busy, they'd insisted that she carry it. Only for emergencies, they'd said.

Was there any emergency bigger than this one?

Ash knew she couldn't linger. She glanced at the door to make sure no one was watching from the hallway.

She fumbled with the phone's password. Then, quickly, she took a photo of each paper in the folder. It took only a minute, Ash guessed, though it felt more like time stood still. When she was finished, she stacked the papers up neatly, returned the folder to the drawer, and moved some pencils on top of it. That way Ms. Cooper would never guess what she'd seen.

Ash rushed downstairs with the masking tape. When she got back to the gym, she felt for the phone, suddenly afraid it would tumble out of her pocket. Had she closed the camera app? How long before it reverted to the lock screen? It felt like years since she'd been playing freeze tag with her classmates. In just a moment, everything had changed. Now Ash knew she could win the Quiz Bowl. Her place in the school would be safe. So why did she feel unsteady, as if she'd just climbed out of the car after a long ride?

Okay, she hadn't looked at the questions yet. There was still a chance for her to be the good kid everyone thought she was. But who was she kidding? The surest way to keep being a "good" kid was to do this bad thing.

To cheat. In her shoes, would anybody choose what was "right"? Ash wondered.

Ms. Cooper's bright voice broke through Ash's dark thoughts. "Let's get this banner up before the late bus gets here!" she said. She climbed up on the ladder, and Ellie moved back into her spot on the other end. Ash helped them center it over the stage, and Ms. Cooper taped it into place. She strode into the middle of the gym to see how it looked. "Excellent!" she said with satisfaction. "Let the Quiz Bowl begin!" In seventy-two hours, it would be happening right here.

Other kids were starting to pick up their backpacks, filing out of the gym and through the atrium toward the bus circle. At this time of day, there weren't bus lines, so Tilly just kind of vanished into the group. Caden gave Ash a fist bump on his way out, putting on an evil-villain voice and cackling, "The Quiz Bowl shall be yours!"

What does he know? Ash wondered nervously. Was there any way he'd seen her with the answers?

Ash left through the back door—where walkers were

supposed to exit—and made her way home alone. The morning's rain had given way to a dazzling afternoon, and she had to shield her eyes as she walked through the parking lot. It was still cold, but Ash could imagine spring now. Maybe soon she could walk to school without her coat. She took her time, stopping to pet a neighbor's dog and appreciating a moment by herself. Ash was one person at school and a slightly different person at home. Between places, though, she was also different. Was this her real self? she wondered. The person she was when no one was expecting anything from her? She wondered if this Ash was a cheater.

As soon as Ash got home, she remembered something important. It was soccer night. Gracie had been begging for months to join a travel soccer team, and the first practice was today, after dinner. One of their parents would drive Gracie to the next town over to practice at the Dome, a dingy bubble that covered an indoor soccer field. Neither of the McNulty girls had ever been on a team, and their parents were not crazy about the idea. It had taken a while for Gracie to convince their dad that twice-a-week practices wouldn't interfere with her homework. "I'm only in fourth grade!" Gracie had pointed out. She'd complained until she finally got her way.

Ash's mom was on her laptop in the kitchen. "Aisling!" she called out. "Can I make you a cup of tea?"

She was pretty much the only person who used Ash's real name anymore. It had a weird spelling, but Aisling was pronounced just like Ashley, only with an *-ing*. It was an Irish name, meaning not just from Ireland but in the ancient Irish language, which had complicated vowels. Ash had given up trying to explain that to people, though. Just like she had given up explaining why she, at eleven years old, drank tea all the time. It was another Irish thing.

Ash left her backpack in the hallway and sat down across from her mother. There was already a mug of tea waiting for her, amber-colored and steaming. Ash poured a glug of milk into it, along with two heaping spoonfuls of sugar. "How was your day?" her mom asked, still eyeing her screen.

"Great," said Ash, though it was anything but. It was like she was reading lines from a script. "How about yours?"

Her mom sighed and rubbed her eyes. "We're getting there," she said.

The McNultys had run an Irish pub in town ever since Ash was a baby, but they were trying something new with it now. The way her dad had put it was, "We want The Gate to be a place people think of for something more than just green beer on Saint Patrick's Day." The Gate was a new name—the place used to be called St. James's Gate, after a place in Dublin, the capital of Ireland. Now it served lunch and dinner, not just bar snacks in the evenings. The food was local, organic, sustainably grown, and inspired by Ireland. It was starting to have a following, which was great—there had even been a story about it in a Boston newspaper. The part that was not so great was that Ash's parents were always working now, basically around the clock, and Ash was pretty tired of trying out new items for the menu.

Ash sipped her tea and watched her mom do

inventory online. She still hadn't looked at her phone, with its photos of the Quiz Bowl questions. It would be safest, she decided, to wait until most of the family left for the Dome. A part of her was dying to see the questions, and a part of her wanted to put it off forever.

There was a strange rumbling in the hallway, a sound that Ash didn't recognize. Then Gracie appeared in a neon-yellow soccer jersey, dribbling a freshly inflated ball. "Not in the house, please," Ash's mom said. Their house was way too small for soccer.

Gracie's smile was radiant. She'd been waiting a long time for this day. "I'm on my way out," she said. She barreled through the kitchen in a blur, her new cleats clicking on the tiles. Ash caught sight of her through the window—you really couldn't miss that jersey—as she made her way to a patch of their yard that was not sopping wet. To her surprise, Ash saw her dad was out there, too.

Her parents came home from The Gate when the lunch crowd had finally died down, but usually her dad spent his afternoons on the phone before the dinner rush, when he often went back to help out the night manager. Today, he was standing in a kid-size goal while Gracie tried to get past him. She was pretty sneaky, but he fended her off until he slipped on a patch of grass, and Gracie scored! He stood up, brushed himself off, and laughed. He seemed happy.

Ash looked away from the window. The only games she ever played with her dad were chess and Scrabble.

Unless you really knew the McNultys, you might not realize that they were from another country—a lot of people didn't even know that immigrants still came to the United States from Ireland. Ash's parents hadn't needed to learn a new language or anything when they arrived years ago, and they had mostly lost their accents. In other words, they blended in. They weren't quite like other people's parents, though, and they didn't always understand the way things worked in their new home. So when Gracie had insisted, "Soccer is important," it took a while for their parents to come around. Even though Irish people loved soccer (which they called football) and games from Ireland were always playing on the big TV at The Gate.

Travel teams had games in other states, and Ash wasn't sure how her parents would drive Gracie to Vermont when they were supposed to be making lunch at their pub-now-restaurant. But that's what American parents did. They packed a picnic and made a day of it. They thought kids needed to start soccer when they were little, so they could get soccer scholarships someday.

Ash's dad rolled his eyes whenever this came up. "Bloody ridiculous!" he'd exclaim. *Bloody* was sort of a bad word in Ireland, but not here. No one said it in Maine unless they were talking about an injury. And no one in Ireland believed that playing soccer was a means to any end except having fun.

Ash's parents constantly reminded their daughters that *school* was the key to success. They'd been lucky to start a new life and business in a new country, but Ash and Gracie couldn't or shouldn't count on the same good fortune, they said. *Education* would pave the way for their dreams. The girls needed to set their sights high, the McNulty parents said. It was their job to get good grades, and Ash always got the job done. Her parents believed a place in the GT class practically guaranteed Ash a bright future, and sometimes Ash heard them bragging about her on video calls with her grandparents in County Galway.

But Gracie wasn't really doing what she was supposed to. She had never even made it onto the honor roll. So why were their parents letting her join this travel team? It was going to distract her from everything important. Ash didn't understand. Were they giving up on Gracie? Her parents knew what was at stake, and so did she.

The McNultys had gone to college, but it wasn't the right kind of college. At least, not according to Jane, who had a book that listed all the American colleges in order from worst to best. Jane wanted to go to one of these schools someday, since that was the way to become an astronaut. "We need to start planning now," Jane had said recently, showing Ash the book. "If you don't go to one of these colleges, you can't go into space. You can't do much of anything. You might end up flipping burgers."

Ash had seen her parents flipping plenty of burgers. It didn't seem that bad, though Ash knew she was supposed to set her sights higher. Yet there was Gracie, heading off in the wrong direction, and their parents were going along with it! It all seemed a little unfair.

In any case, everyone talked over Ash during their rushed dinner. "I hope I don't have to play goalie," Gracie said. "I mean, defense wouldn't be that bad. But I want to be one of the players who scores!"

Ash's mom cautioned, "Gracie, you need to play where the coach tells you to play," and Gracie grimaced. Ash was much better than her sister at following directions.

Ash's dad broke in. "You are pretty fast," he said. "Maybe you'll end up on the front line. But I think it might be a while before you're a starter . . . you have a lot to learn before then."

Ash was pretty fast, too, actually. In gym class, she

ran the mile faster than any other girl in her grade. It was probably on her report card, but Ash knew her parents wouldn't care. They'd just be looking at regular subjects like science and math. At least Ash would have a Quiz Bowl victory to her name by the time they saw her B minus.

Once they were all finished, Ash's mom ushered Gracie out to the car. The house was quiet when they left for the Dome, and Ash's dad had to deal with a call about bread delivery, so Ash picked up her backpack and headed to her room. It had pale pink walls and a heap of toys in it, from back when she was little, but her mom had promised that this summer they would update the room for a junior high girl. Ash wanted to use chalkboard paint on one wall, but she was still waiting for a firm answer about that.

As far as her dad knew, Ash was starting her home-work. But when she heard the clattering of the pots being washed and the loud Irish rock her dad liked to listen to while cleaning up, she finally looked at the phone.

The Quiz Bowl questions were all there, organized neatly by category as if for Trivial Pursuit. To be safe, Ash would need to learn them all, and there wasn't much time. Luckily, memorizing was one thing she was good at. No metaphors or theorems, no abstract thinking, nothing too creative.

Ash covered the answers, tested herself on the questions, and got to work.

Chapter Five

By the time Friday rolled around, Ash had a terrible headache. Her brain was overstuffed with random information that she reviewed ferociously, over and over again. It was as if her mind was overheating.

How many arms does a starfish have? she prompted herself during Morning Meeting. *Five.*

True or false? Dalmatians are born with spots.

False. Dalmatians are born white—their spots appear later in life.

If Ash had thought that having the answers was the answer to all her problems, well, now she knew better. Having the answers caused a whole different problem: a paralyzing fear. What if she forgot them? What if— after this amazing stroke of luck—she slipped?

People could tell that her attention was someplace

else. "You with us, Ash?" Ms. Cooper asked. Caden had somehow become her spokesperson, so he said, "She's just nervous about tonight." Ash was grateful to him, even if he did spill his water all over her backpack by mistake.

She dawdled on her way to Mr. Lopez's, lost in an endless conversation with herself.

How many bases on a baseball field?

Four. That was a trick question, because you had to include home plate.

How many presidents on Mount Rushmore?

Also *four*! At least that was easy to remember.

In Mr. Lopez's room, she wasn't the only kid thinking about the Quiz Bowl. Jane had a glassy stare, as if she'd been up too late, and Olivia wasn't even there. Sebastian looked around the table and said what they were all thinking. "Did she stay home to get ready? No fair!" You didn't need to be one of the GT kids to be in the Quiz Bowl, but pretty much everyone expected them to do well. All of them wanted to win.

"All right," said Mr. Lopez, sighing. "I know it's a big

day." He knew better than to start them on anything new today, so they were left to do more planning for their Island Projects. Jane had sketched out a design for Moon Island, though it looked more like a plan for building an actual moon, it was so complicated.

"Can you tell me the size of Ganymede and Callisto?" Jane asked. Ash knew, now, that these were two of Jupiter's moons. She looked up the numbers online, pretending to be absorbed in this busywork so Mr. Lopez wouldn't ask her about that rewrite. The problem with metaphors, she had decided, was that you either got them or you didn't. She was one of the ones who didn't, and Mr. Lopez knew it. Would a rewrite really change that?

Ash dodged Tilly until the end of the day, when she was back with Ms. Cooper for social studies. Ash couldn't concentrate—she could hardly sit still. When her gaze wandered toward the window, she found that Tilly's eyes were fixed firmly on her. Just watching. Or . . . looking through her. Ash shuddered. Did Tilly know how to blink?

Ash rushed home after school, and if soccer night had been all about Gracie, tonight was all about Ash. Her mom was home early, and there was lasagna for dinner! After gulping it down, Ash put on her most comfortable fuzzy sweater and braided her hair. Then she reviewed the questions one more time, jumping from category to category.

Six missions have landed on the moon.

In Greek mythology, *King Midas* turned everything he touched into gold.

Ambidextrous means *able to use both hands equally well*.

Ash was ready. Not even a robot could beat her in the Quiz Bowl, she thought, no matter what Tilly said. She dared to smile at herself in the mirror. For weeks, she had been doubting that she was really smart at all, but she'd been smart enough to get this far. If she didn't have a brain freeze, this was going to be her night. Maybe everything was going to be okay.

"See you guys there!" she called out to the rest of her family. Gracie and her parents would walk over together, but Ash needed to be at school before them. Mrs. Shepard, the principal and master of ceremonies, liked to go over the rules in advance.

When Ash arrived, the school parking lot was already filling up. The gym floor was lined with folding chairs, Ms. Cooper's banner was bathed in light, and the tables for the cookie buffet stretched across the base of the stage. Mrs. Silver was behind one of them, wearing a headset and directing foot traffic as people arrived with trays of baked goods. She sorted the cookies, sold the tickets, and steered newcomers in the right direction. The Quiz Bowl was the highlight of her year.

Mrs. Silver threw her arm in the air when she noticed Ash, as if she were introducing a celebrity on TV. "The returning champion, folks!" she proclaimed. Ash was a little bit embarrassed and a little bit proud. She waved to Mrs. Silver as she climbed to the stage.

Up there, it felt like being behind the scenes before a big performance, even though the curtain was already up. A school custodian was straightening the cloth that covered a long table. Behind that, someone's dad was pinning small microphones to kids' shirts. "Oh, here you are, Ash," he said as if he knew her. "Let's get you all set up."

While the buzz in the gym grew louder, Mrs. Shepard gathered the contestants around her to explain what would happen next. The second graders would go first, then the third, all the way up to the fifth graders. Then, once each grade had a champion, the top kid in each grade would face off against each other. First graders were welcome to watch, but they didn't compete. It was too much pressure on them, Mrs. Shepard explained, at such a young age.

Ash noticed her family come in through the back of the gym and settle into chairs right next to Jane's mom, Jill Chapman-Haynes, who—unlike Ash's parents—preferred for kids to call her by her first name. Jill was small and very energetic—she used her hands a lot as she spoke to the other McNultys. She had taken Ash hiking, hosted her for Halloween, and found the best coding camp for the pair of girls last summer. Now Ash felt a pang of shame. Just like Ash's parents, Jill had high hopes for tonight. But Jane didn't have a chance, and both of them would be disappointed when it was all over.

Mrs. Shepard was still talking. When the second graders began their round, she explained, the older contestants would wait in the wings. No one in the audience would be able to see them, and Mrs. Shepard reminded them that they needed to be quiet. "Treat each contestant as you want to be treated," she warned. "We all want our answers to be heard."

Before the Quiz Bowl started, the contestants gathered in groups by grade. Ash recognized a lot of the younger kids, and the fifth graders, of course, were mostly people Ash knew well. Here were Sebastian, Lane, and Jane—it turned out Olivia's family was away for the weekend. Here was Sammy Silver, because his mom always made him compete. Here was Ellie, who tried hard but didn't get far last year, with a pair of boy-and-girl twins Ash didn't know. And here was . . . Tilly? Ash couldn't tell if what she was wearing was a T-shirt or a dress. She stood alone in a corner, her foot tapping nervously on the floor, and Mrs. Shepard beamed when she noticed her. "*This* is the way to get to know a new school," she told everybody else. "Just jump right in and get involved!"

Jane glanced at Ash. Kids wouldn't see it that way, her eyes said.

Ash nodded but looked away quickly. It was hard to pretend, right now, that she and Jane were on the same team. Did friends do what Ash was about to do? That was one question she definitely didn't want to answer.

The second graders sat down at the long table as Mrs. Shepard started sound checks. Then the lights dimmed, and the parents' chatter dropped to a few whispers. "Ladies and gentlemen, boys and girls," Mrs. Shepard said warmly. "It is my honor to welcome you to this year's Quigley School Quiz Bowl!" Like every year, she emphasized that this event wasn't about winning or losing but about bringing the community together to celebrate—and share—knowledge. She praised every student who had the courage to take on this challenge. She invited everyone to enjoy the cookies. She reminded them that they were supporting a good cause, as the money raised tonight would support many of Quigley's field trips, including the fifth grade's upcoming adventure at Funtown.

As the second-grade competition began, Ash positioned herself in a dusty corner backstage. It looked like she was cheering on the younger kids with Jane and Lane, but she was really going over the answers one last time. What if they flew out of her head?

In tennis, love means *zero*.

Carson City is the capital of Nevada.

Harry Potter's school is *Hogwarts*.

She paid more attention when it was time for the fourth graders to compete, because whoever won would probably be onstage with her in the final round.

Mrs. Shepard's voice was getting hoarse. "Who was the first Black American baseball player in the major leagues?" she began. The McNultys' neighbor, Ben, knew that answer—Jackie Robinson—and about a thousand others. It took a long time for him to edge out a girl named Violet, but he got it with a math question: "Find

the value of seven cubed, or seven to the third power."
When he answered 343 without a moment's hesitation,
he jumped out of his seat. The fourth grade had a winner!

At that point, Mrs. Shepard thanked the fourth
graders and encouraged the audience to take a quick
break. As they scattered, Ash settled into her place
at the long table, right between Jane and Tilly. She
tapped her microphone to make sure it was working
and searched for her family in the crowd. Gracie gave
her a thumbs-up, and Ash took a deep breath. "You can
do this," she told herself. "It's almost over."

Actually, though, the hardest part was just starting.
Now Ms. Cooper was asking the questions—that had
to be why she had them ahead of time, Ash realized.
Ms. Cooper beamed at Ash and asked her first question, from the arts and literature category. "According
to legend, what was the name of King Arthur's sword?"

"Excalibur," Ash replied quickly. She smiled back at
Ms. Cooper, but it felt more like she was baring her
teeth. What if Ms. Cooper found out what she'd done?

She was always so nice that Ash felt extra awful about tricking her.

The next category was science, and of course Jane nailed it. She knew that the sun was made mostly of hydrogen, and that ROM meant "read-only memory" to computers.

Sebastian was the first fifth grader eliminated, to everyone's surprise. In his rush to answer, he mixed up waxing and waning moons and left the stage to a smattering of polite applause. Soon Ellie followed, then the girl twin. Ash wasn't supposed to clap, but she winked at Ellie as she exited the stage.

When the questions shifted to music, Lane was up. "Please identify the musical family that includes the xylophone," said Ms. Cooper. Lane drummed the table as he said "Percussion," showing off his knowledge of instruments and making the audience laugh at the same time.

Sammy Silver was not so lucky. "Please name a musical instrument with the name of a geometric figure," Ms. Cooper asked him, and he couldn't come up with the word *triangle*. Ash almost rolled her eyes. Even a first grader would know that! But it was painful to see the expression on his face as he trudged down the stage steps to face his mom.

Tilly never faltered, to Ash's surprise, though she had trouble with the microphone.

"Could you repeat that answer?" Ms. Cooper asked her gently.

Tilly spoke up extra loud. "There are *eighty-eight* keys on a piano."

When the category switched to popular culture, the boy twin tripped up on "Name the two sisters in the movie *Frozen*." A little kid in the audience called out "Anna and Elsa" just as the boy said "Anna and Gemma." In spite of the assistance, he was out.

Now the fifth-grade competition was down to Ash, Jane, Lane, and Tilly. When Ash's turn rolled around again, her question was "Who sang the song 'Yellow Submarine'?"

"The Beatles," she said, remembering how her family had played that song on a car trip last summer. It felt good to know the right answers, even if she'd learned them the wrong way. As the number of contestants dwindled, Ash felt a familiar flush of accomplishment. This was the feeling she'd been missing. Right now, she didn't *Need Improvement* at all.

Jane was impressive with her knowledge of old movies. "*Titanic* won Best Picture in 1998," she said definitively.

But Lane slipped up on the name of the actor who played Jefferson in *Hamilton*, and suddenly it was down to the three fifth-grade girls and a fourth-grader named Ben.

Ash looked at her family again. They weren't chatting with Jill anymore but sitting quietly, focused. They would be so proud of her. They would tell her grandparents all about it, and soon everyone in their town in Ireland would know. Ash dared to imagine herself sharing her report card, maybe even telling her parents the truth about what was happening in school. After tonight, they wouldn't be mad, right? Gracie whistled and yelled, "You've got this, Ash!"

Jill was literally on the edge of her seat, as if everything depended on Jane's next answers. Maybe it really did, Ash thought, remembering those college books Jane had showed her. What happened to kids who only got second place?

Suddenly Ash wondered if Tilly's family was here. Who was cheering her on? Now that the end of the Quiz Bowl was closer, Ash was feeling generous. She peeked over at Tilly to give her an encouraging smile, but Tilly was staring at her strangely again. In her T-shirt or pajamas or whatever it was, Tilly looked as if a breeze might carry her away.

Ms. Cooper said, "Our next category is sports," and Ash's heart sank. Under normal circumstances, this was not her strongest category—but luckily these circumstances were not normal. Ash straightened up.

Tilly knew the name of the Olympic swimmer who had won the most gold medals ever. Jane knew the last winner of the Triple Crown. Ash named the field events in a track meet, though she pretended it took a minute to remember them. "Javelin . . . discus . . . and shot put," she said. And then it was Jane's turn again. The audience grew quieter as the tension rose in the room. Mrs. Shepard could say whatever she wanted, but this was definitely a competition.

"Which sports make up a biathlon?" Ms. Cooper asked Jane.

Jane said three sports: "Biking, swimming, and running." Did she not hear the question? Jane, of all people, knew that *bi-* meant two. As in bicycle, with two wheels, or binary, her favorite kind of code, with only two digits. And when Ms. Cooper prompted, "Is that your final answer?" Jane didn't backtrack. It was like she didn't realize she needed a lifeline, to borrow from one of the quiz shows Ash had studied on TV.

"I'm afraid that's incorrect," said Ms. Cooper. "The biathlon is a winter sport that combines cross-country skiing and rifle shooting."

Jane's eyes widened. "Oh," she said, "I meant . . ." But it was too late. Ash kind of brushed her elbow as she stood up, but Jane shook her off. She wasn't even *second place*.

Meanwhile, Ms. Cooper was ready with a new category. "We'll finish with some geography questions," she said, and Ash hoped this wouldn't go on for too long. With Jane out of the mix, she could practically taste her victory.

But it turned out that Tilly had some serious map skills. She knew the longest river in Africa, the capital of Peru, and the real name of the Garden State. Ash identified Japan's main island, the European country shaped like a boot, and the capital of Minnesota. They were evenly matched, Ash had to admit. It didn't sound like Tilly's old school was that great. How did she know so much?

A few families tiptoed out of the gym with sleepy younger siblings, but the Quiz Bowl continued.

"Which river runs through Baghdad?" Ms. Cooper asked Ash.

Again, she pretended to think. "That would be the . . . Tigris?" she said.

"Very nice," said Ms. Cooper, forgetting for a moment that they weren't in her classroom. Tilly frowned at this breach of protocol, and maybe she was still thinking about it when Ms. Cooper came at her with another challenge. "Please name all the Great Lakes."

Ash guessed that Tilly was trying to remember that handy mnemonic device everyone learned at some point. But if you couldn't remember the word *HOMES*, you weren't going to remember all the lakes, and Tilly didn't. "Um . . . Lake Superior, Lake Erie, Lake Michigan . . . ," she said, and she couldn't go any further. In spite of her strong start, Tilly just faded away.

After that, the rest was a blur. Fourth-grade Ben was gracious when he stumbled on his second question, and the audience erupted, first for him and next, more loudly, for Ash. The repeating champion! She walked to the center of the stage to shake Ms. Cooper's hand and accept her prize, a plush snowy owl with wire-rimmed glasses. Mrs. Silver led the crowd to its feet for a standing ovation, and Ash felt like they were applauding for more than just this one night. They were applauding because she was—and always had been—one of Quigley's stars.

It was her night. It was exactly what she'd hoped for, and more. From here, she could rebuild what she'd lost. She could talk to her parents. She could hold her head high for the rest of fifth grade. She could almost cry with relief.

There was only one problem. When the McNultys left the gym, there was still a kid outside in the shadows, waiting for a ride home. It was Tilly, with her arms wrapped around her chest in the growing cold. Ash passed by, following her family, and offered sincere congratulations. "Great job!" she said brightly.

Tilly scowled. "Yeah, thanks," she said without returning the compliment.

Then she lowered her voice, narrowed her eyes, and said something only Ash could hear: "I know what you did. I know how you won."

Chapter Six

One time in PE, someone had passed a basketball to Ash when she wasn't paying attention. Suddenly it slammed into her stomach and she was gasping on the ground. That was when Ash learned what it meant to have the wind knocked out of you. It wasn't just that you were out of breath—it was that all the air was squeezed out at once, in one big gush, and it really hurt. That was exactly how Ash felt now, with Tilly's words echoing in her ears.

In PE that time, Ms. Patterson had stopped the game while Ash staggered to her feet, and the other kids had stood in a circle around her to make sure she was okay. But no one else had seen or heard Tilly, and Ash's family thought she was more than okay right now. They thought she was on top of the world!

It was dark now and much cooler than it had been earlier. The McNultys walked down the school driveway together, heading toward home. "You did it!" Gracie shouted, doing a little dance. "Two years in a row!"

Ash's mom slung her arm across Ash's shoulders. "Nicely done, Aisling," she said quietly. Her praise felt important, and Ash leaned into her mom for warmth.

The whole way home, Gracie kept up her recap. "How did you know all those things?" she asked. "I felt so bad for Jane. And what about that new girl? Tilly? Even I can name the Great Lakes!" Ash didn't want to think about Tilly right now. She didn't want to think about anything if she could help it. She listened to her sister and squeezed her snowy owl, the identical twin of the one she'd won last year. Within fifteen minutes of arriving home, she was asleep.

When she woke up, Ash was happy. Well, at least until she sank back into her pillows, remembering the end of last night. People might think she was some sort of genius now, but Ash could not believe she had been so stupid. She had no idea how Tilly knew the truth. No one had been nearby when she found the answers; Ash was sure of it. She retraced her steps in her mind, but she came up with an empty classroom every time. What would happen if Tilly told? As soon as Monday, people might know that Ash was a cheater and a fraud. And the big news wouldn't just be that she, Ash McNulty, had stolen the answers and basically lied to the whole school. The bigger news would be that Ash McNulty was never that smart in the first place. Who ever would have guessed?

Ash hugged her owls and tried to calm down. *What can Tilly really do?* she asked herself. Would Tilly accuse her after she'd been at Quigley for only a few days? And, if she did tell, would anyone believe her? There wasn't any evidence, since Ash had deleted the photos. And Tilly was so new that people wouldn't trust her. *Maybe this isn't a major disaster*, Ash thought. So she got out of bed, arranged her owls on top of her dresser, and went downstairs for breakfast. The bright morning sun lit up the whole front hallway and, for the first weekend since she didn't know when, Ash wouldn't have to memorize any random facts today. Knowing that gave Ash a burst of energy, almost as if she'd had a shot of espresso.

Saturdays were complicated in the McNulty household. Ash and Gracie were old enough to walk to school alone, but they weren't old enough to stay home alone all day. Since Saturday was the busiest day of the week at The Gate, Ash's parents took turns going to work.

Soon her dad would leave to run the morning staff meeting, but he was unpacking the dishwasher when Ash walked into the kitchen. "I can't wait to tell the crew about the Quiz Bowl," he said. "Bet you could teach them a thing or two at the pub's Trivia Night." His eyes sparkled with pride, and Ash wasn't sure if he was even serious. Did he actually think she could compete against grown-ups? "Maybe if you're on my team . . . ," she said doubtfully.

Ash ate some cereal, then got dressed. Most Saturday mornings, she and Gracie went to the farmers' market with their mom. This time of year, it was inside an old brick building that used to be a paper mill, with vendors' stalls under soaring arched ceilings. There weren't a lot of fresh fruits or veggies in the cold months, but there were plenty of farmers selling local foods like bread and cheese, not to mention all kinds of crafts. While their mom chatted with vendors and scouted out ingredients for the new spring menu, Ash and Gracie loved to roam on their own, trying all the free samples.

"I'll meet you right here in twenty minutes," her mom said when they arrived at the market. She was already eyeing some golden beets. Ash nodded, inhaling the scents of celery and cinnamon. This week, she and Gracie sampled tiny cups of cider and dipped cubes of bread in fancy salad dressing. Ash dared Gracie to try a pickled pepper. "It's so sour!" Gracie said, spitting it into a napkin. The girls rounded a corner and headed to one of their favorite stalls, where a farmer sold socks and mittens woven from alpaca fur. Ash had never been able to talk her mom into buying them, but she and Gracie always tried things on.

Gracie was modeling an alpaca cape when Ash realized that Mrs. Silver was standing right behind them, her shopping bag loaded with leafy greens. She petted a pair of soft mittens before her eyes landed on Ash. "Oh, honey," she cooed. "You were just spectacular last night! I've never seen anything like it. You're a walking encyclopedia!"

Ash beamed. She liked remembering the good parts of the Quiz Bowl. "Thanks," she said modestly. "Sammy did a great job, too."

Mrs. Silver waved the compliment away. "He did his best," she replied. "But seriously—have you ever thought of trying out for *Jeopardy!*?" Naturally, Mrs. Silver knew just how to go about it. She was midway through her lengthy instructions when she spotted Ash's mom in the next aisle.

"Clare!" exclaimed Mrs. Silver, her voice ringing out across the market. "You must be so proud!" She nodded in Ash's direction and added, "What a star! Your Aisling is really going places!"

On a normal day, Ash's mom would have hurried away while trying not to be rude. She was always afraid that Mrs. Silver would rope her into organizing a potluck supper or something. Today, though, her whole face lit up. "Thanks, Elena," said Ash's mom. "It was quite a night." She stood there quietly as Mrs. Silver told her about the *Jeopardy!* prizes.

Ash stored up Mrs. Silver's compliments and her mother's pride as eagerly as she'd stored up the answers for the Quiz Bowl. A voice in her head whispered *Tilly* from time to time, but it was easier to drown it out when she was being praised. After all, this was exactly what she'd won for.

Her dad was in charge for the afternoon, and he took the girls on some errands before he dropped Gracie off for her Saturday soccer practice. They went to the post office, the grocery store, and the dry cleaner. Ash even went along for the ride when her dad dropped Gracie off for soccer. Then, as the van rolled into the gravel parking lot at the Dome, Gracie said, "You should come and see me play!"

"Parents come to practices?" Ash's dad asked. The whole family was still learning the ropes.

"I think so," Gracie said. "I mean, there were tons of parents at the first one. People cheer for their kids and sometimes help with the coaching." They all under-stood what she meant: American parents.

Ash had never been inside the Dome, though she had heard people talk about it for years. It didn't really seem like her kind of place. But Gracie had cheered her on last night . . . "We should go." Ash nudged her dad. "That way we'll know what to do when there's actually a game."

She led the way through a revolving door and felt her ears pop with the air pressure when she emerged into the Dome, which was kind of like a landlocked blimp. The light inside was dim, and the noise was deafening. A couple of teams were competing already, and Gracie was right about the parents. They were even louder than the coaches, shrieking, "Now, Jenna! Take it up the line!" and "No . . . no . . . offsides . . ." and "Shoooot!" Ash was totally out of her element.

When Gracie joined a group of girls dribbling balls around orange cones, Ash settled with her dad in a nar-row space by an air vent. It didn't take long to notice that Gracie wasn't keeping up with the others. Sometimes she'd lose control of the ball and have to run after it.

Sometimes she'd pass it to the wrong girl. And when the team practiced shooting on the goal, Gracie never seemed to make it in. Ash sighed. She wondered, again, why her parents were letting Gracie do this. What if she was wasting her time? Gracie's grades weren't great, and soccer didn't seem to be her thing, either. Did she ever wish for a big win, like Ash's? She wouldn't want Gracie to be jealous, but she did want Gracie to *care*. She wanted her sister to be a girl who was going places, too.

By the time the practice was over, Gracie's face was red and her hair was slicked back with sweat. Ash would have been upset after making so many mistakes, but Gracie just took a long swig from her water bottle and said, "I can't believe I have to wait three whole days to come back here!" Ash didn't get it.

"Hey, when are we picking up Jane for movie night?" Gracie asked in the car on the way home. Most Saturdays, Jane came to the McNultys' for a movie and a sleepover. But it was too awkward to have Jane over tonight, Ash had decided. If their places were switched,

Ash probably wouldn't want to hang out, and the last thing she wanted to do was review every moment of the Quiz Bowl. Or do more research about moons.

"Oh, she was busy," Ash told Gracie. The lie just slipped out of her mouth before she could do anything about it. Now that she'd started lying, would she ever be able to stop?

Sleepovers with Jane always involved ice cream, and Jane's favorite flavors had a "core" inside—a different flavor at the center of the container, like caramel buried inside vanilla. If Ash were a pint of ice cream, she'd be like one of those. On the outside, she was a flavor everyone loved—say, chocolate. Inside, though, there was a new core of something sour, like pickled pepper. The whole point of winning the Quiz Bowl was to stop having secrets, but now there were new secrets about the Quiz Bowl, and they made Ash feel like she was going rotten.

When the end of the weekend arrived, Ash sat down at her desk and cleared away a stack of Trivial Pursuit cards. Then she opened her backpack and took out her assignment notebook.

Animal Farm rewrite was the first thing on the list. Well, at least she could cross that one off. No need to do that now, or pretend she wanted to, since she had won the Quiz Bowl. Now Mr. Lopez would know she was smart enough to see the metaphors, even if she had messed up on the essay.

It was the next item that left her feeling like the wind had been knocked out of her all over again. *Report card*.

Yes, it was still in her closet, in a bin with some stuffed animals, and for a couple of days Ash had forgotten all about it. Now she pried the cover off the bin and lifted out a gray bunny who had probably never expected to help her hide anything. Ash unfolded the report card and looked at it again. The B minus shone as if it were printed in neon, and when the honor roll was finally posted in the school's front hallway, Ash knew the absence of her name would glow even brighter. How could the winner of the Quigley School Quiz Bowl miss the honor roll?

Ash was out of excuses. She had to bring this report card, signed, to school. But there was just no way she could show it to her parents, even after putting it off for all this time. Why hadn't she thought this through? They were extra proud right now, and if they saw this report card they'd be crushed. Ash herself was crushed. This wasn't who she wanted to be. It wasn't who she *was*!

She wouldn't get it signed by a parent. Because now that she was on a lying streak, she had a new idea. It wasn't smart, but she was in survival mode.

She would sign it herself.

It was so easy to scrawl her mom's name in black pen—it didn't look like real words, but her mom's real signature didn't, either. Ash stuffed the report card in the front pocket of her backpack and zipped it as tight as she could. Once she delivered it to school, everything would go back to normal.

On Monday morning, Ash took so long to get ready that Gracie left without her, and Ash arrived at Quigley at the same time as four school buses full of kids. She glanced around anxiously, but she didn't spot Tilly in the crowd. Once people noticed Ash, they treated her as if she had won a gold medal. Caden stopped traffic when he spotted her, pausing to do a mock bow and say "All hail!" on his way up the stairs. "Great job, Ash!" one of Gracie's friends yelled over his head. "You rock!" said Olivia, who had missed everything but clearly been filled in.

Suddenly there was a lime-green parka at Ash's elbow, making a double-dazzle with Ash's own. "Twinsies!" said Ellie, as usual. She was very cheerful for someone who had been eliminated so quickly on Friday night. "Way to go!" she added.

Just like Ash's parents, Ellie's parents were from another country—Vietnam—and, just like hers, they stressed that school was super important. *Are they ever disappointed in her?* Ash wondered. Ellie had never done well in the Quiz Bowl, and she wasn't even in Mr. Lopez's class. What did they say when they saw *her* report card? Ash checked the zipper on her backpack pocket to make sure it was still closed tight.

Ash and Ellie climbed side by side to the second floor. Just as they got there, another girl pushed past them without saying anything—which wasn't unusual, except that it was Jane. She was wearing headphones, and she acted like she hadn't even seen Ellie or Ash. Was it Ash's imagination, or did she leave a cold breeze behind her?

Ellie said, "She was that way on the bus, too. Didn't take the headphones off. Maybe she feels bad about the Quiz Bowl?"

Ash swallowed. She'd see Jane in language arts, and it could be tricky.

She felt extra nervous as she walked into Ms. Cooper's room, but there was still no sign of Tilly. Ash took her coat off and hung it next to Ellie's. She left her assignment notebook on her desk, careful not to cross over into Caden's territory, then removed the report card from her backpack pocket and slipped it into Ms. Cooper's in-box at last. Ms. Cooper would share it with Mr. Lopez.

The class moved into Morning Meeting, and one of the announcements was about the Quiz Bowl. "Friday's event brought us way over our dollar goal for Quigley field trips," said Ms. Cooper. "And the winner

of the Quiz Bowl was our very own Ash McNulty!"
Ash blushed as everyone applauded. She even felt good
about her part in the fundraising. With money from
the Quiz Bowl, the whole grade would be going to
Funtown in one of those fancy buses with plush seats
and personal TV screens. They'd do a little bit of science once they got there, but it was mostly for fun. Ash
had never even been on a roller coaster, and she'd heard
that the one at Funtown had three loops.

When Ms. Cooper took attendance, Ash realized
she'd had a stroke of luck: Tilly was absent. Ms. Cooper
led the class in a morning greeting, then directed them to
the Word of the Day, which was an easy one. "*Bereft* . . . ,"
said Ash when she was called on. "I think that's . . .
feeling like something is missing? Or lost, maybe."

"You got it, Ash!" Ms. Cooper said enthusiastically.

Caden added to his tally sheet. "Sixteen for sixteen,"
he whispered.

Ms. Cooper adjusted the shades in the classroom,
and when Ash saw the brilliant blue sky, she had a flash
of hope. Maybe Tilly wasn't just absent. What if she

wasn't coming back? There had been that mix-up with the desk and the loss at the Quiz Bowl—what if her family had decided Quigley was the wrong school for her? Ash might never see her again.

That daydream lasted until Ash left for language arts with Mr. Lopez. She skipped down the upstairs hallway alone, enjoying the special freedom that came from being a GT kid. In junior high, she realized, everyone would have the kind of independence she had right now. There would be no more moving with the whole class in a long line, no more staying with the same teacher all day. She thought of Ellie and the other kids from Ms. Cooper's class. They were going to love this!

Ash went down the stairs and came around the corner on the first floor, lost in thought. But just as she arrived at Mr. Lopez's door, she saw someone leaving the front office with a tardy slip.

Naturally, it was Tilly.

Chapter Seven

illy looked around the empty hallway and beck-
oned for Ash to follow her to the only place where
they could have some privacy: the bathroom.

As soon as the door closed behind them, Tilly leaned
against a sink and folded her arms, her eyes burning
into Ash. "Why did you do it?" she whispered so no
one would hear. For once, she wasn't hiding under a
hood. It might have been the first time Ash saw her
whole face, and it was furious. Her hair was in uneven
pigtails that bobbed up and down.

"Do what?" Ash asked. She kept her voice low,
though she was pretty sure no one else was in here.

"Don't act all confused," answered Tilly. "I told
you—I know what you did. I know how you won. I saw
you with your phone."

"My phone?" Ash repeated. No one had been there that afternoon; she was sure of it.

Tilly exhaled, irritated. "Yes," she hissed. "Taking pictures of something. I could tell you were sneaking around. Was it for the Quiz Bowl? But why? You wanted to win that badly?"

Ash felt cornered, though she wasn't admitting anything. "Wait, what? Where were you?"

Tilly said, "Remember we were in the gym, hanging the banner? And then Ms. Cooper sent you upstairs? But then she sent me upstairs, too, to tell you to bring some more markers. I got a little lost, but when I finally found the classroom, I caught you in the act. I mean, I didn't know what you were doing at first—I just saw you taking pictures with your phone, super fast. I put it together later. I'm smart, see."

It was possible, Ash had to admit. Once she'd started taking pictures, she didn't notice anything else. Now she was speechless.

"So you knew the questions ahead of time?" Tilly pressed.

"And the answers," Ash said softly.

"Well . . . you got what you wanted," Tilly said. "The big win."

Ash couldn't even look at her. "Did you tell Ms. Cooper?" she asked.

"No," said Tilly.

Phew. "Okay, good."

"Well . . . not yet."

Ash's expression went from relieved to stricken. "You can't! Please!"

Tilly retorted, "I knew the answers, and I would have won if you hadn't, like, sprinted ahead of me because you got a head start. It's not fair!"

But Ash had *needed* the Quiz Bowl, and what was it to Tilly?

"Why do you even care?" Ash said. Tilly was fierce now, so unlike the timid girl she'd taken on the tour.

"I'm new?" Tilly said, like it was obvious. "And if I won, I'd make a good impression?"

Ash swallowed. Another way to make a good impression, she realized immediately, might be for

Tilly to turn Ash in. To appear not just smart, but honest. A good citizen. Ash couldn't let that happen.

"I can explain . . . ," she said desperately. She'd tell Tilly the whole story if she had to.

Tilly shook her head and cut her off. "I didn't know the answers. I didn't have fans in the audience, cheering me on. I don't go to your special class. But I knew just as much as you did, maybe more! You bet I'm going to tell someone. I just don't know who. I don't even know how things work around here."

Tilly's words bounced off the tiled walls of the bathroom, and suddenly Ash felt overwhelmed. "I need to go," she said urgently. "Mr. Lopez . . ."

She couldn't even finish the sentence. If Tilly said one word—to anyone at Quigley—Ash's whole world would come crashing down. Tilly didn't understand who she was dealing with. Ash was . . . what had Mrs. Shepard said? Someone really special. A leader and a role model, one of our very best. She had the golden ticket! Her friends, her parents, even other people's parents had the highest hopes for her. And even if

Ash's secrets had grown heavy, even if they were eating away at her inside, that was still better than having everyone know the truth.

"Okay, well, see you at lunch," said Tilly. Was that a threat?

Blindly, Ash made her way to Mr. Lopez's room, where everything was peaceful and normal. Jane, Lane, Sebastian, and Olivia were already seated around the big table, working on some logic puzzles that Mr. Lopez liked to give them as warm-ups on Monday mornings. "Hey, champ," said Sebastian.

Mr. Lopez winked at her. "Heard you had a big night on Friday!" he said.

"She was on *fire*," Lane confirmed.

Olivia and Jane had their heads together, trying to make sense of their puzzle. "The passenger isn't in a train station that begins with the same letter as their name," Olivia read out loud. "So we can cross off those people . . ."

Jane noted the information on a grid, trying to narrow down which one of seven imaginary people was about to take a train trip. "Hey, Ash," she said without looking up. "Great job on Friday."

"You were awesome, too," Ash gushed, friend to friend.

"Those were some seriously tough questions," Jane replied. "I mean, we didn't even review all those categories!"

"Right?" said Ash.

Jane glanced up from her logic puzzle. "But you seemed to know a lot of the answers."

What was she saying? Ash froze.

"So . . . were you practicing without me?" Jane asked. Was she mad . . . or hurt? Olivia edged away.

"Well . . . yeah . . . ," Ash stammered. It wasn't like they'd agreed to compete as a team. "I mean, weren't you also practicing without me?"

"Not as much as you were, I guess," said Jane. She bit back anything else she might have wanted to say, and Ash settled awkwardly on the opposite side of the table until Mr. Lopez gathered them together as a group.

He settled into his place, folded his arms, and leaned

back in his chair almost like he was one of the kids. "Okay, folks, we'll come back to the logic this afternoon, before math. Just wanted to get the cobwebs out of our brains after the weekend, you know?" He told them a little about taking his new puppy to obedience school on Saturday. Mr. Lopez's puppy was not gifted or talented, and she had a tendency to chase the other students around her class.

Eventually he circled back to their work. "We're going to wrap up our unit by writing in our journals," he told the group. "One more way to think about *Animal Farm* . . ."

Ash wanted to scream. Would they ever be done with this book?

"Here's where you'll start," he continued. "In *Animal Farm*, remember, the pigs take over the farm from the humans. They promise to make the farm a better place for animals, but by the end they are treating the animals even worse than the humans did in the first place. As you know, the pigs have collected too much *power*."

He emphasized that word and paused to let it sink

in. "Here's what I want you to consider. Is it possible to have too much power? What might too much power do to a person . . . not just to a pig?"

Jane's hand shot up. "How are you going to grade us?" she asked. "Is there a rubric?"

Mr. Lopez smiled. "You know I don't grade your journals," he said. "This assignment is just for you, a chance to explore some of the ideas we've discussed. To delve in, you might say. So . . . does this book mean anything to you as a fifth grader? Does it connect to any thoughts or experiences in your real life?"

Ash closed her eyes. She was willing to bet that Ellie and Caden didn't have to answer questions like this for Ms. Cooper. She had absolutely no clue what to write. She drew the two pigs, Snowball and Napoleon, on top of her paper while she waited for a good idea to come to her. In spite of everything, she still had good ideas sometimes.

Who had power, anyway? The president. The principal. Her parents. Maybe the mean kids on the playground at recess. Now that Ash was in fifth grade, they were gone, but there were some older boys who'd chased Ash and Jane all over the playground when they were younger. They had a kind of power, even if no one outside school could see it.

Did any other kids have power? The answer came to Ash as soon as she asked the question.

Actually, all the kids around this table had a kind of power. They had a special position at Quigley, and it came with extra privileges. Like how Mr. Lopez was letting Ash do that rewrite, just because. And hadn't she been feeling thankful that she could walk from class to class on her own? It was all because she did well on that test a long time ago. Ash didn't want to think about what would happen if she had to take that test again today. Would Tilly ever get to try it? Probably not.

She'd never asked for any of this, but Ash liked being special. And when she thought she might lose her place, she'd done a bad thing to remain one of the "good" kids. Did that mean she was abusing her power, like the pigs in the book?

She knew what Tilly would say. Ash had cheated

her way to victory in the Quiz Bowl because no one would ever suspect her. Wasn't that taking advantage of her reputation? Using power that maybe she didn't deserve in the first place?

Ash gulped. One way or another, Tilly was going to tell. And then what? Ash blinked back tears. She'd risked everything to keep this from happening, and now it was about to happen anyway. Everyone would know that Ash McNulty was not the person they thought she was, and now there was no way out. She really wanted to be that person, the girl who was going places. But the person she really was—uncertain and afraid—was burning with guilt and shame.

So how would a "good" kid get out of this mess? Ash wondered. Not just a good student, but a kid who was good in every other sense of the word.

If she was one, Ash realized slowly, a good kid might admit her mistake.

No, she thought reflexively. How would that even work? She couldn't, like, make an announcement to everyone who had come to the Quiz Bowl. Could she just confess to the people who would care the most, like Jane? Ash wasn't sure that would count.

Then she thought back to her special place at Quigley. Grown-ups listened to Ash. They respected her. She had a kind of all-access pass to the adults in the building, and that gave Ash an idea.

She didn't write much before Mr. Lopez collected their journals and moved into a lesson about Latin roots in English words. When language arts was over, Ash lingered just behind Jane and Olivia in the downstairs hallway and then, when they were almost to the stairs, she said, "Oh no! I forgot my pencil case." At that, she wheeled around and headed back to Mr. Lopez's room.

Mr. Lopez was greeting his fourth graders, and Ash loitered in the doorway until she caught his eye. He looked at her curiously, but she made a gesture toward the nurse's office. Now he knew she was going to see the nurse for some reason, and he could tell Ms. Cooper when she called to find out why Ash hadn't returned upstairs.

Ash slipped out of Mr. Lopez's view and hurried right past the nurse's office before she lost her nerve. The next door was the main office, where the school secretary, Ms. Caruso, was talking to a second grader. Her eyes lit up when Ash walked in. "Ash McNulty!" she said. "I hear congratulations are in order!"

"Thanks," Ash said. "Um . . . is Mrs. Shepard here?"

"As a matter of fact, she is," Ms. Caruso said.

"Can I . . . see her? I need to . . . talk to her," Ash said haltingly. It felt like her mouth was full of mashed potatoes.

Ms. Caruso acted as if kids asked to see the principal on a regular basis. "Right this way, dear," she said, leading Ash past the copy machine and away from the bustle of the main office.

Mrs. Shepard was at her desk, staring at a computer screen. She lowered her glasses when Ash walked into the room. "Lovely to see you, Ash," she said.

Ash had to stop her before she said anything nice. Her eyes were filling up, so she saw Mrs. Shepard as if she were looking through a windshield on a rainy day, but she managed to get her words out without crying. She couldn't pretend for one more second, so she just blurted it out.

Ash said, "I need to tell you something. About the Quiz Bowl."

Chapter Eight

I t felt terrible to spill the whole story, but Mrs. Shepard was crisp and kind. "I'm so glad you came to me," she said after Ash confessed. "I promise that this is the first step toward making a positive change."

Ash could not imagine one positive thing that was going to happen now. While she trembled next to Mrs. Shepard's desk, the principal called both of her parents. "I'd like to invite you for a meeting this afternoon . . . ," she began. "I'm afraid I have some difficult news." Ms. Cooper and Mr. Lopez would be giving up their lunchtime to join them.

Mrs. Shepard put down the phone and looked at Ash. "The best plan, I think, is to stick to your usual routine for the rest of the morning." She smiled so warmly that Ash wondered, for a second, if she was even in trouble. Was she going to get away with cheating just because she was a Talent Development kid?

"It's going to be okay," Mrs. Shepard went on. "It was brave of you to tell me. And together we can figure out the consequences."

So there would be consequences. Ash knew that she deserved them, but her heart sank as she walked away.

In Ms. Cooper's room, the rest of the class was taking a science test. Ms. Cooper whispered, "Feel free to use this time to catch up on your work, if you need to." She didn't seem to know, yet, that Ash McNulty was the reason she'd be missing lunch today. Tilly's head was bent over her test, pretending she didn't notice Ash, but that didn't fool Ash for a second. It comforted her a tiny bit to know that, by the time Tilly decided to rat her out, it would be too late.

Ash turned to the book she kept in her desk for emergencies. In Narnia, Edmund was chasing promises made by the White Witch, but they'd all turned out to be lies. He was Ash's least favorite character in the book, but she felt some sympathy for him right now. His whole life was about to be ruined by one huge mistake. At least she wasn't the only one.

Ash was the last kid out of the room for lunch, which meant that no one was watching as she peeled off the end of the line and made a turn into the front office. "They're waiting for you in there," said Ms. Caruso curiously.

Ash felt like she was about to walk into a magic cabinet, the kind she'd seen at a magician's show one time. The magician had chosen a volunteer from the audience, locked her inside, and said "Abracadabra!" with a whoosh of his wand. When the magician opened the cabinet, the volunteer had vanished. Now the Ash McNulty that everyone had always known would be disappearing from Mrs. Shepard's office in three, two, one . . .

Ash's parents were facing the principal's desk, not even making small talk, as Ash came in behind them. "Have a seat, Ash," Mrs. Shepard said, pointing to a chair. Her mom turned around, her eyebrows lifting in surprise, and Ash realized something that made this whole moment even worse, if that was possible.

Her parents had thought this conference was about Gracie.

Mr. Lopez walked in with a tablet under his arm. He nodded at Ash and said, "Hey, kiddo," in the dark tone you might use if someone had experienced a family tragedy. Which this was, in a way.

Ms. Cooper arrived at the last minute, saying, "Sorry to be late. I had to trade playground duty . . ."

Mrs. Shepard nodded and began. "We have a situation," she said to the group. "It seems that there were some . . . irregularities at the Quiz Bowl." She led into it gently, but there was no getting around the truth. "Ash was able to access the questions and answers in advance, so her victory was guaranteed."

Ash's dad shook his head. "She cheated?" He looked at his daughter. "But . . . she wouldn't need to. Sometimes we think she knows more than we do." He smiled, but he seemed confused, and Ash's face flushed with embarrassment. Was this really happening?

Ms. Cooper swallowed. "Ash, how did you get the questions?"

She might have figured it out already, but Ash was going to have to say it out loud. She looked at the floor and admitted, "I saw them in your desk. When I went to get the masking tape. And I . . . took pictures of them, so I could memorize the answers."

"I see," said Ms. Cooper. To Mrs. Shepard, she added, "When I sent Ash to my desk, of course, I never imagined . . ."

"No one imagined," said Mrs. Shepard somberly. "This is not the behavior we expect of Quigley students."

Ash's mom was quiet while her dad kept speaking. "I don't understand. That's not like Aisling. As I said, she's way beyond most kids her age." He seemed stuck on that idea.

That was when Mr. Lopez piped up. He put his tablet on Mrs. Shepard's desk and said, "Well, as you could see on her report card, Ash had some struggles last quarter." He scrolled to pull it up so everyone could see.

Ash's parents looked at each other. "Her report card?" Ash's mom asked.

"It would have come in your mail," said Mr. Lopez. "Though of course you can get the most up-to-the-minute grades in Gradebook."

Gradebook was a way to track kids' grades online, and Ash knew that Caden's parents were obsessed with it, but her parents never checked it. For one thing, they didn't need to, at least not for Ash, and for another thing they thought of it as something that American parents did. Helicopter parents, Ash's mom called them.

"We're still waiting for her report card to arrive," Ash's mom said.

Ms. Cooper turned to Ash. "Didn't you just return it, signed, this morning?"

"Signed by who?" asked Ash's dad.

"By you?" Ms. Cooper said. She was thoroughly confused, and now there was another thing Ash had to admit.

"I signed it," she said quietly. "I didn't want you to know. I didn't want anyone to know."

So it all came out, and of course her B minus was only the beginning. They talked about *Animal Farm*, and abstract thinking, and the rewrite that hadn't happened. They talked about theorems in geometry and the way she had forged her mom's signature. Ash might have soared at the Quiz Bowl, but now she was crashing hard.

"What were you thinking?" Ash's mom asked, about all of it.

Ash took a deep breath. "I was thinking I could make it all better if I just won the Quiz Bowl," she said, sniffling. "Everyone would remember I was super-smart, so the other stuff wouldn't seem so bad." It was the truth, but it felt like a lie when she said it. It was the world's worst plan, and Ash had been sure it would change her life.

Disappointment hung in the air like smoke. "I just can't believe . . . ," her mom started to say.

Ash's dad shook his head. "You've made a hames of it, so you have," he said to Ash.

Mr. Lopez's head snapped up. "A hames?" he asked.

"A mess," said Ash. Her dad slipped into Irish slang sometimes when he was upset.

Mrs. Shepard cleared her throat. "There will be time for explanations," she said. "But I brought you all here to talk about next steps. Ash has many apologies to make, and we will talk about disciplinary measures. I must say, though, that I don't see this entirely as a disciplinary matter. It's an opportunity to consider whether we're giving Ash what she needs at Quigley."

"Agreed," said Mr. Lopez, jumping right in. "I think we have a bigger issue here than the Quiz Bowl. I have always respected Ash's work, and I have always loved having her in my class." He smiled at her as warmly as possible, under the circumstances. "But there's no need for her to be on the fast track, so to speak, forever. Maybe Ash would benefit from slowing down a bit."

Ash didn't like where this was going.

"Slow down in what way?" her mom asked.

"Well," said Ms. Cooper delicately, "I would welcome the chance to teach Ash all day, for instance."

All day with Ellie, Caden . . . and Tilly.

"And we do cover the same concepts in every fifth-grade classroom," Mr. Lopez added, "though some have the chance to get into greater depth."

"Sounds like we're all on the same page here," Mrs. Shepard chimed in. "It could be just the right time for Ash to take a step back, make sure she grasps all the end-of-year material. After all, we want for Ash to finish fifth grade strong."

"Step back by leaving Mr. Lopez?" her dad clarified. He was not happy.

"Yes," said Mrs. Shepard. "Not for long, necessarily. But long enough for her to catch up and to sharpen her skills. Then we can discuss whether she's ready for the faster pace again. Or whether she can just pick up with the advanced group at the beginning of sixth grade."

Mr. Lopez added, "Ash will still flourish outside my program. Ms. Cooper's classroom is differentiated, which means that she offers appropriate challenges to each one of her students."

No one was asking Ash.

Ash's mom turned to Mr. Lopez, pushing back on

his idea. "She's really benefited from the small class size in your room ... ," she began.

"And we want her to be ready for junior high," her dad continued. "I hear the GT program there is very challenging." He'd heard that from Jane's mom, Jill, who said it was one of the best in the state.

Mrs. Shepard's tone was patient. She gestured to the teachers and said, "I think we all feel that she'll be in the best place if she leaves the Talent Development class for the time being." Somehow, in that instant, there was a decision. "Let's make sure to keep the lines of communication open."

Ash wondered what it would be like to be with Ms. Cooper all day long. There would be nothing for her to "catch up" to—she'd mostly be waiting for other people to catch up to her. She'd have a chance to reread the whole Narnia series, probably.

Meanwhile, she was going to be without her GT friends or teacher—her school family, with their memories and their in-jokes and their ability to understand one another when other kids did not. Mr. Lopez's puppy would learn to sit and stay, and Ash would never hear about it. She was being cut loose, and as she finished the week or the month or the year, whatever it was, in Ms. Cooper's classroom, Tilly would be watching the whole time. She'd had no idea, until a few minutes ago, that this was even a possibility.

Finally she got a chance to speak. "Do you have any questions, Ash?" Mrs. Shepard asked.

"Well, yes," said Ash. "I mean . . . is that the consequence?" If there was anything else, she wanted to know.

Ms. Cooper sighed. She couldn't let anyone off the hook for something so major. "I also think it would be appropriate for you to miss the field trip to Funtown," she said with regret.

"And you'll need to apologize to the parent group that organized the Quiz Bowl," said Mrs. Shepard. "They will be disappointed by the way you undermined their hard work."

Ash nodded because she didn't dare to speak. She felt like she was going to throw up. She didn't mean to undermine anyone's hard work! Now she was going to miss her first trip to a real amusement park, maybe her only chance to try riding a roller coaster. And how could she ever apologize? The Quiz Bowl would never be the same. Long after Ash left Quigley, Mrs. Silver would still be thinking about how to keep kids from cheating their way to victory.

Ash was allowed to go home with her parents, not that it made her feel any better. Her mom and dad were silent with shock, and Ash huddled under a blanket on the couch. Her mom sort of disappeared until it was time for her to leave for The Gate. Eventually Gracie came home, and Ash heard a murmured conversation in the kitchen before Gracie helped herself to a snack. She brought two bowls of pretzels to the living room and sat down beside Ash on the couch. "I heard what happened," she said. "I am so, so sorry." She handed her sister one of the bowls.

"Me too," said Ash. "I mean, I'm *really* sorry."

Gracie put her feet under Ash's blanket. "So you can't go to Funtown?"

"No," said Ash, shaking her head. They both knew their parents weren't taking them on a roller coaster anytime soon. Their family didn't do theme parks. "And that's not even the worst thing. Did Dad tell you I have to leave Mr. Lopez?"

Gracie thought about that. "It's still school, Ash," she said. "Ms. Cooper's class isn't, like, a vacation."

"I know," said Ash. "But still." Her sister didn't get it. For some reason Ash thought back to this morning's Word of the Day. Back then, she was someone special. It was as if she'd been wearing bright garb—a fancy costume—and now she was naked. Bereft.

Their dad steered clear of them until he was rushing out the door. "Your mother will be home before dinner," he told them. "You can have half an hour of screen time after your homework is finished." His voice sounded normal, but he didn't make eye contact. Ash was waiting for a zinger, and it came as he put on his coat. "I thought you were smarter than this, Aisling. Now your whole future is on the line."

That was the beginning of their conversation, and also the end.

Ash bristled as the door closed behind him. She already felt so awful . . . would it have hurt him to be a little nicer? She pulled the blanket all the way up to her neck.

"That's not even true, Ash," Gracie said. "You've seen him interview people to work at The Gate. He doesn't ask them how they did in fifth grade."

She had a point.

For a moment, Ash's misery gave way to a flash of anger. She was just a kid! Kids made mistakes, some small and some big. Gracie made mistakes all the time, and no one pestered her about her future. For all Ash knew, her future might still be bright. If only she could get through tomorrow.

Chapter Nine

Ash stayed in her bedroom for most of the night, pretending to do her homework. Was she supposed to do her math for Mr. Lopez now? A part of her wanted to do it, just to keep up with the GT class, but another part of her never wanted to see it again. When she did look at it, the triangles and circles all blurred together. Her phone bleeped just as she'd finally given up and started drawing in her notebook. Ash had a text, and there was only one person, apart from her family, who had her number. Jane.

Ash put the finishing touches on her sketch of a horse, making sure the mane was just right. She took a deep breath before daring to read the message, but the text was friendly enough. Jane didn't seem to suspect anything was wrong, and if she was still upset about the Quiz Bowl, she didn't mention it. **Missed you this afternoon,** Jane wrote. **I did some more work on Moon Island. We're almost ready to make some models!** Ash didn't text back. There was nothing she could say.

Gracie gave her a pep talk on the way to school the next day. "It's going to be fine, Ash," she said. "Like everything else, this is going to blow over." Anyone who overheard them would have thought Gracie was the older sister.

"I hope so," Ash said. Even though nothing else would be normal today, she was still early for school. She slunk past the main office with her head down and hesitated before she stepped into Ms. Cooper's room.

Yesterday, Ash had seen a new side of Ms. Cooper. Her smile had been pressed down into a straight line, her gaze unblinking. Today, though, the usual Ms. Cooper was back, as sunny as ever. "Good morning, sweetie," she said when Ash arrived. "Let's make today a good day, okay?"

This was not at all what Ash expected. "Okay," she said. Her eyes swam with tears again.

Ms. Cooper's voice was soft. "Listen," she said. "Can I give you a piece of advice?"

"I guess so," Ash said.

"Don't be too hard on yourself," said Ms. Cooper. "Don't make this worse than it has to be. You did something wrong, and you're going to make it right. You admitted it, and you'll apologize. What else can you do? You can only do your best, Ash. You can only look ahead. And who knows? Maybe something good can come out of this episode. Try to keep an open mind, okay?"

Her face lit up with a smile, and Ash did her best to match it, even though this was the most confusing advice she had ever heard.

"Honestly, I'm thrilled you'll be with my class all day," Ms. Cooper continued. "You're going to grow a good deal more than you think."

Ash had her doubts, but she nodded politely, and then her classmates started to arrive. Caden tried to get her attention by poking her with the eraser end of his pencil, but Ash sat stiffly, pretending to be wrapped up in her book. Only a careful observer would have noticed that she never turned a page.

How would Ms. Cooper explain why she was switching classes? How would the other kids react when they found out? Would anyone even speak to her now? As Morning Meeting began, Ash was petrified.

She barely hung on until the Word of the Day, her very last chance to shine. Luckily, she'd heard of a *din* before.

"*Din* . . . is it dinner?" asked a girl named Charlie.

"It's definitely not lunch," Caden offered, and some other kids cracked up.

Ash raised her hand. "I think it's a noise," she said.

Ms. Cooper beamed, and Ash had a millisecond of pride and relief until Tilly chimed in. "A loud and confusing noise," she clarified.

Her glance—and her correction—burned Ash. If Ms. Cooper didn't say something soon, Tilly would.

Just before it would usually be time for Ash to get up and leave, Ms. Cooper made her announcement. Her voice was super excited, like someone in the class had just won a million dollars. "Ash McNulty will be joining us for language arts and math today," she said. "I know you'll all make her feel welcome." It was an invitation, not an accusation.

"Oh yeah!" said Caden, pumping his fist in the air. "About time!"

Ellie leaned over Caden's desk to catch Ash's eye. She said, "We're way more fun than Mr. Lopez's class. You'll see."

Ash waited for the kicker. But Ms. Cooper didn't say *why* she was staying, and no one even asked. People just started getting ready for language arts like nothing had happened, ruffling through notebooks and searching backpacks for their homework.

Was that all?

Ash felt like she was sitting on a stage, blinking in a spotlight, yet no one had bought a ticket for her show. She'd been expecting public humiliation, but Ms. Cooper kept all her mistakes private. Now Ash wondered if she'd been worried over nothing. Why would Ms. Cooper ever tell the whole class how Ash had won the Quiz Bowl? Weren't the other consequences enough?

She breathed deeply and closed her eyes for a second. Maybe this would be all right.

Ash had expected to be the star of a show today, but as language arts began, she realized she was more like the audience. Now that she'd be here full-time, Ash observed the class, and her classmates, with new eyes. There were kids in this room who she barely knew, and who barely knew her. They had already shared a school year's worth of time together. How was she supposed to get to know them now, near the end of the year? In some ways, Ash was as new as Tilly. And speaking of Tilly—why was she wearing flip-flops today?

Ms. Cooper moved to the middle of the room and crossed her arms. It had to be some sort of invisible signal, Ash thought, because the buzz of conversation stopped. "Today, friends, we are going to write a story together using our figures of speech," she explained.

Would she be doing figures of speech until the end

of fifth grade? Ash wondered. So much for learning anything new.

Ms. Cooper didn't sit down, like Mr. Lopez did. She walked around the room, which kind of forced people to pay attention. "I'm going to get us started with the first line, okay? We'll start with a bit of hyperbole—or exaggeration—and then we'll add sentences using different figures of speech."

She started the story dramatically, throwing her hands up in despair. "So . . . this morning I overslept, I burned my toast, I put on mismatched socks, and I missed the school bus," Ms. Cooper said. "It was the *worst morning of my whole life.*"

"Sounds like every morning for me," joked a girl named Naomi, who was sitting next to Tilly.

"Thank you, Naomi," Ms. Cooper said as she wrote the first line of the story on the board. "How about you add the next line? Can you give me some personification?"

"Sure," said Naomi, caught by surprise. "My dog howled when I finally walked out the door."

That wasn't right.

Ash raised her hand, but Ms. Cooper called on Will, one of Caden's friends. "That's not personification, is it?" he asked. "Because a dog *does* howl? So you're not, like, giving human qualities to something inhuman? You're giving dog qualities to a dog."

Ms. Cooper nodded. "So, let's do a quick edit. Who can help?" she asked.

Ash waved her hand higher this time, but again Ms. Cooper looked past her to call on Charlie.

"How about ... the wind howled when I finally walked out the door?" she said.

"Nicely done," said Ms. Cooper.

When it was time for a simile, Ellie came through with, "The rain was like a cold shower on my head," and Ms. Cooper even gave her the chance to add an extra one. "I ran to the bus as fast as an Olympic sprinter."

The class advanced to alliteration, then onomatopoeia. "The thunder went *clap*!" someone added, and the whole class giggled. Why was that funny? Was Ash missing out on some inside joke? She felt a pang of missing her other class, where she always knew when to laugh. What were they doing right now? she wondered. When would she see them again?

Ms. Cooper's voice broke into her thoughts. "Ash, could you add an idiom?"

Ash's mind went blank. Did Mr. Lopez teach this one? she wondered. "Um . . . ," she sputtered. "I don't think we covered this . . ." She could feel herself blushing. She was supposed to know it, and she had no idea.

To her relief, no one connected idioms with idiots. But then something worse happened: Tilly raised her hand.

"Remind us what an idiom is?" Ms. Cooper prompted her, as if she were some kind of expert.

"It's an expression that can't be understood by just the literal meaning of the words," Tilly explained smugly. "Like 'it's raining cats and dogs.' Or someone was 'under the weather.'"

"Right! So let's add a great idiom to our story," Ms. Cooper continued, and Tilly said, "Once I started sprinting, getting to school on time was a piece of cake."

The class murmured its approval—people always liked a mention of cake—and everyone moved on. Except Ash. *She* was supposed to be the smartest girl in this class. And if she wasn't, who would she be? Ash imagined herself gradually going invisible. Tilly would grow brighter and bolder as Ash just faded away.

When lunchtime rolled around, Ash stuck with Ellie. She ate a slice of school pizza at Ellie's table and followed her out to the playground, breezing past Jane and their usual spot on top of the Pyramid. Ash and Ellie snagged side-by-side swings and leaped off them when they got high enough. By the time the bell rang, Ash was elated from that feeling of flying. She'd forgotten Jane for a moment, along with all her troubles.

Without thinking, Ash then followed Ellie right past the Pyramid on her way to the spot where Ms. Cooper's class would line up to return inside. Too late, she saw that Jane and Olivia were still there, hanging back for a moment, and now Ash was too close to ignore them.

Jane spoke up at once. "Ash?" she said. "You're in school today?" She sounded genuinely confused, so

Ash guessed that Mr. Lopez had not leveled with his class. "Where were you during language arts?"

Ash should have prepared for this moment—after all, she knew it was coming—but she found that she had no words. Mr. Lopez obviously didn't know what to say, and Ms. Cooper hadn't told the whole story, so Ash avoided it, too. "I just decided to stay with Ms. Cooper today," she said uncomfortably. "I . . . couldn't get away." It was yet another lie, and Jane knew it.

Ash expected a cross-examination, but another voice rang out above her before Jane could prepare her line of questioning. Tilly was in the upper levels of the Pyramid, and she'd heard their whole exchange. Now she flipped down and perched on the bottom rung.

"You can't believe a word Ash says," Tilly told Jane. "She *had* to stay with Ms. Cooper. Because of what happened in the Quiz Bowl."

Jane was baffled. "What happened in the Quiz Bowl?" she asked. "What do you mean?" She looked at Ash, then at Tilly.

Ash braced herself.

"Well, she cheated," Tilly said bluntly. "She stole the questions ahead of time, so she knew all the answers. You and I never had a chance."

Jane turned to Ash, her eyes wide. "That's how you knew all that stuff we never even covered?" She paused to take it in. "But why would you do that? Why didn't you tell me?"

"Tell you what?" Tilly asked. "The answers? No, she kept those for herself. For some reason, she really wanted to win."

"Everyone wanted to win, Tilly. Even you," Ellie pointed out.

Tilly retorted, "Not enough to cheat."

"It's a long story, Jane," Ash began, sighing. "It started way back with *Animal Farm*. No one knew it, but I was totally lost . . ."

Then another bell rang, and Ash was saved. Now there were only about ten seconds left to line up. "Sorry . . . ," she said, convincing no one and hurrying away as fast as she could, leaving the rest of them behind. She made it to Ms. Cooper's line just as the doors opened and the class started filing in. More than anything, Ash wished she could hide for the rest of the day.

Chapter Ten

The next morning, Caden nudged her halfway through science and pointed to the crumpled piece of paper in his palm. It could be a note, Ash thought, though with Caden you never knew. He might have some other reason for holding on to a scrap that looked like it had passed through a dozen hands. "Hey, Ash," he whispered. "Is it true?"

The note said, *Ash McNulty wrote all the Quiz Bowl questions herself!* Ash wasn't sure if she should laugh or cry.

"Well, did you?" Caden asked. "Did you cheat?" He looked almost disappointed.

Ms. Cooper was eyeing them. "Not like that," Ash said out of the side of her mouth. It was the truth, if not the whole truth.

Later that afternoon, when they were coming back from gym, Ms. Cooper's class passed Mr. Santorini's class in the hallway. Mr. Santorini was one of the oldest teachers at Quigley, and he was a little bit loose with the rules—he did not object when Sebastian, who was one of his students, stepped out of line to talk with Ash. "I heard you had an alliance with the new girl to win the Quiz Bowl. What's her name . . . Tilly? How did you do it?" Sebastian didn't seem outraged—more like fascinated. Based on their years together with Mr. Lopez, Ash guessed he just wanted to know how she had masterminded such a grand scheme.

Even Gracie had heard some version of this story. "Want to know what Ben told me?" she asked Ash at dinner that night. Ben was their neighbor, the fourth grader Ash had beaten out for the snowy owl. "He said that you and Tilly both had people feeding you answers from the audience. And then Tilly's person disappeared."

Ash laughed. "Just . . . vanished?"

"Yep," said Gracie. "With a puff of smoke."

Tonight they were having dinner at The Gate because a group was hosting a birthday party there, and both of their parents wanted to make sure the food was just right. Rather than staying home alone, the McNulty girls were tucked into a booth at the back of the pub with a special meal that wasn't even on the menu: spaghetti and meatballs and french fries.

The booth's wooden benches had been recently polished, along with everything else inside The Gate. Not that long ago, The Gate had felt like an extension of the McNultys' living room, comfortable but a little shabby. Now there were sleek new tables and chairs in the dining area and silver pendant lights hanging above them. Everything was clean and bright, as if the whole pub had just stepped out of a shower.

Ash dipped a fry in her tomato sauce. "Let people think what they want to think, I guess. That way I'll never have to explain what really happened."

"The stories are crazy, though!" Gracie pointed out.

"People just want to know why I'm in trouble," said Ash.

"In trouble?" Gracie asked. She took a sip of lemonade.

Ash thought back to that awful meeting in Mrs. Shepard's office. "I mean, everyone acted like it was for my own good, but it sure feels like a punishment to me."

"To be in Ms. Cooper's class?" Gracie said. "Lots of kids love her."

Yes, that was true. Ash backtracked a little. "I love her, too. It's just . . . I don't know what to tell people. They think I'm paying the price for something, and they want to know what it is."

"It's none of their business," Gracie said. "You don't have to tell them anything."

Ash considered that. "Yeah . . . people think it is, you know? Like I lost something that everyone else wishes they'd had in the first place."

Gracie's gaze was steady. "Honestly, Ash?" she said. "If they knew what you really did, they'd think you got off easy."

When Gracie got up to go to the bathroom, Ash was left alone with those words. She was missing the

Funtown trip. She'd been cut off from her special place at Quigley. Wasn't that enough?

Now that she was alone at the table, Ash noticed some other things that had changed at The Gate since the last time she'd been here. The background music was different now, more Irish harps than bagpipes. The big TV at the end of the bar was switched off. Where there used to be a map of Ireland on the wall, there was now a big chalkboard with the day's specials in her mom's careful writing. And along with the classic burger, there was now an asparagus risotto on the menu. Was the asparagus from the farmers' market? Ash wondered.

No matter what was new to eat, though, some things would always be the same here. Their town was small, and it was pretty much impossible to be at The Gate without running into people you knew. Sure enough, someone from the birthday party peeled away and approached Ash's table. "I thought that was you," said Mr. Nguyen, Ellie's dad. "I had to come over and say hello. Ellie will be sorry she missed you!"

The person with the birthday was someone from his office.

Ash hadn't seen Mr. Nguyen since she went sledding with their family over the winter break. Now she felt shy, wondering what he knew. Had he been at the Quiz Bowl? Did he suspect she'd been disgraced? Would she always be so ashamed?

"Nice to see you!" Ash said in the voice she used at The Gate. The McNulty girls knew how to act at their family business, always warm and welcoming. The voice made her seem extra mature, and Mr. Nguyen recognized it. "You girls are getting so grown up," he said. "Almost ready for new adventures in junior high, right?"

Why did parents always want to talk about school?

Was it because they thought Ash had no other interests?

She nodded, and Mr. Nguyen continued. "Ellie just loves having you in her class all day," he said. "And her mom and I are pleased, too. She'll learn so much from you!"

Ash's heart sank. Mr. Nguyen might know her reputation for being smart, might even have seen her win the Quiz Bowl two years running. But now that she was with Ms. Cooper full-time, she could see that other kids looked up to Ellie. Ash's friend might not be a Talent Development kid, but she had a special place all her own.

Ash was relieved when another adult from the party came toward Mr. Nguyen. Gracie came back to the table, and the girls mulled over what to order for dessert. They had just settled on the chocolate tart with ice cream when Ash realized, to her horror, that the other adult was Jane's mom.

She ducked her head. "Just move a little to hide me, okay?" she said to Gracie in a low voice. For years, Jill had been like an extra parent to her. What did she think of Ash now?

Jill hadn't seen the girls, but soon she spotted Ash's mom. It wasn't an ideal time for conversation, as Ash's mom was helping the people in the party sort out how much they owed for the meal, but Jane's mom didn't seem to notice. "I love what you've done with the place," she said, gesturing around. "So sophisticated now!" Ash caught the expression on her mom's face. It wasn't completely happy, more like fake happy. Like she didn't appreciate the compliment. Was there a hint in it that The Gate had not been so great before?

Then Jill launched into one of her favorite subjects: summer enrichment programs. Last year, she'd found a coding camp for Ash and Jane, and this year she had something even more challenging in mind. Ash's mom was juggling several credit cards and a couple of other conversations, but Jill persisted in telling her all about it. Ash could hear her voice above the rest of the noise—the din!—in the pub.

"I found the perfect robotics program for the girls, Clare," said Jill. "I'll send you all the registration details as soon as I get home. It's at the community college, and technically it's for high school students, but I think I can get them in." Jill had tons of connections.

In their booth, Gracie made a face at Ash. "Robotics?" she said. She'd spent last summer at a kayak camp, where she took swimming lessons in the morning and paddled along the coast all afternoon. On the last day of camp, Gracie had insisted on signing up for the following year.

"I guess so," Ash said without enthusiasm. While Gracie explored coves and shorelines, she and Jane would be in a lab somewhere, writing code to make Lego figures run around. It was cool, yes, but did it qualify as "summer vacation"? There wouldn't be much time for, like, sitting in the backyard with a Popsicle and a stack of library books. And would Jane ever forgive her for the Quiz Bowl? Ash would never do robotics without Jane, but she wasn't sure she wanted to do it *with* Jane, either, not the way things were going right now. The girls hadn't spoken since Tilly told the truth.

Ash shuddered. She pushed any thought of Tilly to the back of her mind.

When their chocolate tart was ready, Ash's mom brought it to the table. "We're almost ready to go," she told her daughters. "I know it's getting late. Once the party settles up, the staff can handle closing for the night."

She turned to Ash and asked, "Did you see Jill? She has some great ideas for summer."

Ash spooned up some ice cream. "I don't know about robotics, Mom," she said. "Could we think about something else?"

"Let's discuss it at home," said Ash's mom. That was her polite way of saying that she didn't want to discuss it at all. "I just think you could learn some valuable skills in a camp like that . . ." She trailed off.

"Valuable skills for making robots?" Gracie said, giggling. "Not many people need that skill, Mom."

"Valuable skills for junior high math and science," Ash's mom said evenly. "The academics are about to get a lot more serious for Ash."

It was as if her mom was speaking in a code that only Ash could decipher. Yes, the academics were probably harder in junior high, but was that all Ash's mom really cared about? Ash had a feeling this was actually about making sure she returned to the GT program. The principal had left that door propped open, and Ash's parents were determined to find the way back in. Just this morning they'd been all over Ash, checking Gradebook and following up. Had she done her homework? Had she received any new grades? They were just like the helicopter parents they used to complain about.

Ash knew there were kids who pretended to be sick so they didn't have to go to school. She'd heard of tricks for doing it, like holding a thermometer up to a light bulb to create a "fever," yet she'd never really understood why you'd want to miss school in the first place. Now she totally got it, because she didn't want to be there herself. She didn't belong anywhere now. And there was always that danger that the real Quiz Bowl story could tumble out at any minute.

All morning, she watched the classroom clock. When would it be lunch or, better, recess? Ash longed for recess, and she wasn't usually that kind of student. Twice during music, she asked to be excused, and took her time wandering to the bathroom. Her footsteps echoed in the empty hallway. She stared out a window, eager to be on the other side of it. To breathe fresh air.

When recess finally rolled around, Ash followed Ellie into a makeshift kickball game, the first of the season. The field was a sea of mud now that the snow was gone, but there was just enough room on the bluetop to fit all the kids who wanted to play. Ash was stuck in left field, but anything was better than running into Jane. It was fifth grade versus fourth grade, and the action was intense.

Will was the pitcher, and he was pretty solid. He could get the ball right down the middle of the plate, leaving hopeful fourth graders to boot it to the outfield—where someone would catch it cleanly and end the play. But then a couple of fourth graders aimed the ball just where no one could get it. In no time, their team had three runs and Will had runners at first and second base.

Ellie gathered the outfielders together and said, "Spread out! Their best kicker is up next!" Ash and the others scattered to the farthest edges of the bluetop.

To Ash's surprise, the fourth-grade star was her sister! Will pitched, and Gracie made contact on her first try. Her kick was strong and sure, and the ball sailed way above the head of the girl who was playing second base. "Look alive, guys!" Will shrieked.

Ash was fast, though. Speed was her secret superpower!

She ran backward to the edge of the bluetop and reached as high as she could, plucking the ball from the air just as it was arcing toward the ground. "Out!" she called.

"Yes!" some voices chorused. There were high fives across her team, as Ash McNulty had saved the inning. Ash gave a no-big-deal smile and tossed the ball back to Will, but she could detect a change in the air. At that moment, she'd earned a new kind of respect.

When the teams switched places and it was Ash's turn to kick, no one gave special instructions. No one in the game—except maybe Gracie—had any idea what Ash was capable of. The rest of them saw only a smart kid. A Quiz Bowl winner. Someone they thought they knew. Suddenly Ash wanted to show them a different side of herself. More than just her brain.

She got two strikes and a ball, but Ash was patient. Eventually she got a beautiful pitch, slow and right down the center of the plate. She had time to line up her foot with the ball and gather all her strength to whale it decisively. The ball soared over the bluetop and into the parking lot beyond.

Ellie covered her eyes. "Please, don't hit a car . . . ," she said. "Please, don't hit a car." But the kickball came to a stop safely, and Ash took her lap around the bases as her team cheered again. It was a home run!

"Nice going!" Naomi yelled.

"McNulty? Who knew?" added Will.

When the bell rang, Ash's heart was still pounding from her run. Or was it bursting with pride? she wondered. She'd surprised them all, Ash thought, and maybe she'd also surprised herself. How often did her grade play kickball? she wondered. She'd never even noticed before, and now she couldn't wait to try again.

Chapter Eleven

There was still one way she could be the same old Ash—she found it by accident during math time the next afternoon. Ms. Cooper had just reviewed strategies for finding the area of a triangle, and now there was a little bit of in-class practice for everyone. Ash's practice was a set of "challenge" problems in the textbook, the kind she would have done with Jane in her old class. They were extra tricky.

Beside her, Caden was huffing. He filled his cheeks with air and blew it all out at once in a way that sounded exactly like a whoopee cushion. People kind of laughed, because Caden was always making people laugh, but Ash could also see the mess on his paper. There were no answers there, just a heap of eraser shavings and a few gray streaks. Ash used to think of Caden as an enemy, but he was starting to be a friend. She decided to step in.

"Do you want a little help?" Ash whispered. "I'm pretty good at this." His questions were simpler than hers.

"Yeah," muttered Caden. "You're good at everything, Ash."

Was he mad at her or mad at his triangles?

Ash tried again. "No, seriously," she said. "You just have to break it down, Caden. It's one half the base times the height, but you can't start there." Ms. Cooper saw them talking, but she didn't stop them, so Ash went on. "You have to have all your information set up ahead of time. See?"

She showed him how to find the length of the base and the height—the units were squares, since they were using graph paper. "And then once you have it all," she continued, "it's just a little multiplication, like back when we were doing the times tables, with a fraction at the end."

Immediately, she wished she hadn't said that. Caden had been in her third-grade class, too, and he could never get the times tables quite straight. He frowned at his paper and erased something so vigorously that he made a hole.

"So what's the height of this one?" Ash asked, pointing to a triangle.

"Five squares," he said.

"Okay, good. Now what's the length?"

"Looks like . . . eight." With Ash's help, he wrote these facts down, then plugged the numbers into a formula.

She prompted, "So, five times eight . . ."

"Forty," he said, faster than she expected. "And then you put it over two—so you divide it—so it's twenty? Right?"

"Right!" Ash said. She was super positive, like a coach.

Caden scrutinized his paper. "That's it?" he asked.

"Seriously, that's it," Ash confirmed. For some reason, she thought of the kitchen at The Gate. "Think of it like cooking. If you get all the ingredients chopped up ahead of time, it's easier. You don't have to start and stop, or rush off someplace to find an onion. You can just, like, turn on the heat."

Caden pretended he was chopping an onion and mopping his eyes. "I'm crying!" he joked. But he got serious when he turned to Ash. "Thanks!" he said. "That totally makes sense. How did you get so smart, anyway?"

Ash smiled. Who didn't love to hear that?

But she had told Caden exactly what Ms. Cooper had already told the class. Did that really make her smart? she wondered. Ms. Cooper couldn't go over things with every student one-on-one. There were twenty kids in this room, not five like Mr. Lopez had. Would Caden do better in a smaller class? Had Ash? Was *that* why she was so far ahead of him?

Whichever it was, helping Caden reminded Ash that she had once been a responsible, respected kid, and maybe someday she could be one again. That boosted her mood, which was helpful for a person who felt like she was walking on the edge of a cliff.

Too bad her mood came crashing down before the end of the day.

After math, Ms. Cooper gave the class some time to work on their Island Projects. Caden was with Will, and Ellie was with Naomi, and Ash just stayed at her desk, wondering what to do. Ms. Cooper moved from group to group, making sure kids were on task, until she came to Ash. "How is your island coming along?" she asked kindly.

"Well, my partner is in Mr. Lopez's class," Ash explained. "I'm working with my friend Jane." She left out some details, like how they weren't speaking and how all the ideas for the project were Jane's.

Ms. Cooper nodded. "I see," she said. "I'll need to discuss with Mr. Lopez, but I'm sure he'll agree it doesn't make sense to have partners in two different rooms. I think it would be much better for you to find a new partner and get a fresh start. We'll be spending a good deal of class time on our islands now, in order to prepare for Island Night."

"But everyone is paired up already," Ash said. "So . . . should I join one of the other groups?" *That would be so awkward!* she thought with alarm. And how could she guarantee she'd make a great island if she couldn't even pick her own partner?

Ms. Cooper gave her a reassuring look. "Oh no, don't worry! I have a better idea. Someone else in the class could use a partner, and I know the two of you are friends already."

She stepped out of the way to reveal a student who was waiting behind her, wearing patched overalls and a short-sleeved shirt that used to be white. "It's a perfect solution, a win all around," Ms. Cooper said, clasping her hands together. "I was thinking you could work with Tilly."

Ash briefly wondered if she was going to die. People did die of embarrassment, right? How could she go through with this? Tilly had seen her at the lowest moment of her entire life, snapping those pictures in desperation, and then told the whole world. Or Ash's best friend, at least. If she could still call Jane her best friend.

But it was hard to say no to Ms. Cooper, so Ash trudged with Tilly to the other side of the classroom.

They sat down at side-by-side desks, both staring straight ahead in silence, until Ash pulled her desk around to face Tilly's. "I guess we need a theme for the island," she muttered. One of them was going to have to take the lead.

Tilly acted like she'd never heard of this project, even though she wasn't *that* new by now.

"What kind of theme?" she said.

"Like . . . something we're really interested in," Ash replied.

"Such as?"

"I think Caden is doing a Fortnite Island. So every feature on his island—rivers, mountains, whatever—will have something to do with *Fortnite*."

"The video game?" Tilly said in disbelief. "Are you serious?"

"It's what he's into," Ash said. Why was Tilly mocking Caden? She barely knew him.

"So what are you into?" Tilly asked.

Ash didn't want to give Tilly too much information. "I don't know . . ."

"School, obviously," Tilly said. "So . . . we do *School* Island?" Her voice was soaked in sarcasm.

"I have other interests," Ash said defensively.

"Oh yeah? Like what?"

She was impossible. Ash was not going to sit here and tell Tilly, of all people, the things she liked to do when her homework was finished. She liked to draw, she liked to run fast, she liked to reread all the books she'd loved when she was little . . .

All she could do was turn the question around. "What are *you* into, Tilly?" Ash asked.

The new girl shrugged. "Sea turtles," she said. "Solitaire."

Maybe they could work with that. "Sea Turtle Island?" Ash suggested.

"I guess," said Tilly. She opened her notebook and drew a turtle shape. "Like this?" Slowly, they sketched in a few geographical elements, as if it were a real island—Shell Beach, Seaweed Road. But the project required a long list of features, from roads to rivers, plus they also needed to develop a legend for their map or model. Other kids had been working step by step for a while now, so Ash and Tilly were behind.

Suddenly Ash had the same feeling she'd had before the Quiz Bowl, like she was struggling to catch up. And now a new weight was settling on her shoulders, because she knew she had to get a top grade on this project if she had any hope of getting back to Mr. Lopez like her parents wanted. How was it even graded? she wondered. Well, Ash knew you got points for turning in various pieces of the project on time—not good news, since she and Tilly were getting a late start. But what else? How could Ash make sure her island was the best it could be . . . and maybe the best overall?

There would be prizes at Island Night—that was when all the fifth-grade parents came in to see their kids' projects hung in the school's hallways as if in an art gallery. Ash would love to get another prize, the honest way this time. But how would she know what was *right*?

Ash had nothing against sea turtles, but she didn't love this idea.

And she began to despair that she and Tilly would ever make progress, because Tilly never seemed to be in school. On Monday she was late, on Tuesday she left early. When she was there, she sometimes looked like she was falling asleep. Ash did her best to create the legend when there was class time for it, but one of the things they were getting graded on was teamwork. Days raced by with no progress.

Meanwhile, no matter how much school Tilly missed, *she* would get to go to Funtown. On Friday, the parents who were chaperoning came in to review the rules and split the class into small groups. "Each group will have its own T-shirt color," Ms. Cooper explained. "That way it will be easy for us to find each other at the amusement park." She read from a list of names— the blues, the reds, the yellows, the greens—and each group went to stand with its leader.

This was agony for Ash. Once all the colors were called, she'd be the only kid left sitting in her seat. And yes, at some point, she was going to have to tell people why she was staying behind, but she didn't have her story straight yet. So, when the greens stood, Ash stood with them. She walked over and joined the knot of kids around Charlie's mom, smiling as if she belonged there.

Tilly was a green, too. "I didn't hear your name, Ash," she said. "Are you sure you're in the right group?"

Ash wasn't sure if Tilly was being helpful or sly. But she had hit on a question that was consuming Ash: What group was she in? Was she regular or special? Was she smart or sporty? And would there ever be a place with no groups, where Ash could just *be*, away from expectations, blending into the crowd?

Chapter Twelve

Ash had never looked forward to a weekend so fervently. She didn't care if her parents worked all weekend, so long as she didn't have to go to Quigley. This was the Saturday, she decided, that she would use some birthday money to buy herself some fancy chocolates at the farmers' market. She would reread a fun book, maybe *Matilda*. Somehow, she would relax.

And then Gracie caused a crisis by accident, when she mentioned the Island Project at home.

"Hey, how's your island?" she asked on Saturday morning. "I can't wait to see it!" Just like Ash had been last year, Gracie was excited about all the fifth-grade rites of passage that she'd get to be a part of someday—from the Island Project and the Funtown trip to

Step-Up Day and the Manners Banquet. She didn't know that she'd hit on a sensitive subject.

"Good," said Ash, taking a big bite of toast. Her eyes darted over to their mom, who was tidying the kitchen before she left for The Gate. Had she heard?

Yes, she'd heard. "Jane's mom mentioned you were making models," she commented. "All the moons in the solar system, or something?"

Ash swallowed. "Well, I'm not working with Jane anymore. Since I switched classes and all." The two of them still weren't speaking, and Ash had no idea how to break the silence. They might not be friends right now, but Ash didn't want to be enemies.

"Who's your partner now?" Gracie asked.

"Tilly," said Ash.

"Does she even go to Quigley anymore? I never see her at recess."

Ash bulged her eyes out at Gracie, hoping she'd recognize that was a signal to shut up. "Yeah, she's still at Quigley. She's just absent a lot."

Now their mom was extra attentive. "That must make it hard to get anything done. Would you want to have Tilly over to our house?"

"Not really," Ash said in horror. "I've got it, Mom, okay?"

Her mom put a tea bag in a travel mug, poured boiling water over it, and gathered her things to leave. Today she was wearing a light jacket, not her winter coat, and Ash could actually hear birds outside the kitchen window. "Just remember that you need to do your best work, Ash," her mom said on her way out. Like Ash didn't know that already.

She bristled at the idea that her mom thought this was helpful. But when her mom said something even a little bit critical of Ash, it echoed for a long time in her brain, as if her mom had shouted into a cave. She kept thinking of her mom's suggestion. There was no way she was having Tilly over. But Ash did have Tilly's phone number, because Ms. Cooper had made sure that all sets of partners knew how to get in touch. Maybe they could get together someplace else?

Ash really didn't want to see Tilly at all. Even a sleepover with Jane would be better. On the other hand, she had a lot riding on this island. While Gracie got ready for soccer practice, Ash went into her bedroom and closed the door. Her phone was in her backpack, and Tilly's number was written on the back of a worksheet. Did Tilly have a cell phone? Ash wondered. Could she just send a text? She sighed and knew she couldn't risk it. Slowly, Ash punched in the digits.

Tilly picked up right away, but her hello slid from friendly to frigid as soon as she heard Ash's voice.

"Can I help you?" Tilly asked.

"Do you want to meet me at the library?" Ash said bravely. "I thought we should do some work on our island."

"I can't," said Tilly. "My mom's at work." Did she need a ride? Ash wondered. Couldn't she bike there or something? Ash didn't know anything about Tilly's family. She didn't know much about Tilly, either, if she thought about it. Just that she was from Florida and that she'd been either brilliant or very lucky in the Quiz Bowl.

"Okay," said Ash.

She was about to hang up when Tilly said, reluctantly, "Maybe you could come here?"

It turned out Tilly lived right on the way to the Dome, so Ash's dad could drop her off. And while Ash's mom might have asked a lot of questions about adult supervision at a stranger's house, her dad didn't dig too deep. Once he knew Ash was going to Tilly's for schoolwork, it was fine. He pulled into Tilly's driveway and said, "I'll pick you up on the way back, right?"

"I'll text you if anything changes," Ash said.

"Good luck," Gracie whispered as Ash climbed out of the car.

Ash stood in front of the house for a moment, wondering how to get to Tilly. The downstairs was not a house at all, but some kind of a bakery. There was a row of windows above the storefront. Did Tilly live up there? Everyone Ash knew lived in a house. She had never been in an apartment before.

Ash was looking for a doorbell when a woman stepped out and said, "You must be Ash." She looked like Tilly, with blond hair and bleary eyes. She had come downstairs, and now she was heading toward the bakery door. Was she getting them something to eat? She smiled and held the door open for Ash. "Tilly's waiting for you," the woman said. "Thank you for coming."

The thank-you put Ash more at ease. She climbed a narrow set of steps and, when she came to the door at the top, she could hear Tilly calling "I'm in here!" from inside. Ash let herself in.

Tilly was sitting on a striped rug in the middle of a small room jammed with boxes. They'd just moved here, after all. She left Ash standing there, looking for a place to sit, for an uncomfortably long time. There were art supplies strewn across the room, as far as Ash could see. Finally, Tilly cleared some pens and paper out of the way.

"So . . . the island," she said. She wasn't exactly friendly, but she wasn't openly hostile. "I hope you don't mind, but I redrew it."

Ash did mind—until she saw that Tilly had drawn a much larger sea turtle on a piece of posterboard. It looked a lot better, almost lifelike, and they'd have to use posterboard for Island Night anyway if they were doing a map instead of a model.

"Nice," Ash said. She took the assignment sheet out of her pocket. "So we have to add some mountains, a capital city . . ."

They worked on it for a while, but it felt like just that: work. This wasn't the way Ash had imagined the Island Project would go, back when she was Gracie's age. It wasn't fun, even if Tilly had markers in every color and a great set of stencils. Mostly, they just colored things in without talking. Ash wondered about the woman she'd seen downstairs and when she was coming back with the treats.

She inhaled deeply. "It smells so good in here," she said. Like apples and cinnamon, or maybe brown sugar. Ash had food on her mind, for sure.

Tilly smiled a little. "I think they're making pies downstairs." When Ash didn't reply, Tilly filled her in. "My mom works there. It's a new place, and she's the head baker. Didn't you meet her? She's here but not here, if you know what I mean. She pretty much works all the time."

Ash knew what Tilly was getting at. Not everyone's parents were always around. "My parents work a lot, too," Ash said. "They have a pub. Or they had a pub. It's turning into a restaurant. Like, it's fancier now."

"Oh," said Tilly, nodding. "Okay." She was a little less prickly outside of school. She was wearing shorts and a T-shirt, still a bit optimistic for the end of April, but otherwise normal. For the first time, Ash wondered if Tilly wore weird clothes because she'd been unprepared for Maine weather when she moved.

"So where do you go when they're working?" Tilly asked.

The question caught Ash off guard. "I hang out with my sister, I guess," she said.

"Oh yeah. Gracie. In fourth grade, right? Well, I have to stay right here," said Tilly. "My mom's still trying to figure out things for me to do. Back in Florida, I went to an after-school program."

Ash nodded. She wasn't used to talking about

childcare arrangements, but at least now she knew why Tilly couldn't hop on her bike and go to the library. For all Ash knew, she might not even have a bike.

Tilly stood up and stretched. "Are you hungry?" she asked.

"Kind of," Ash said. She could practically eat a refrigerator.

"I think I'm going to make some brownies," Tilly announced. The kitchen was just steps away from the rug, and Ash guessed the whole apartment was smaller than the first floor of her own house. Did Tilly and her mom share the bedroom? she wondered. Tilly hadn't mentioned that anyone else lived here, like a dad.

Tilly melted some chocolate on the stove. She piled butter and sugar into a bowl, then started the mixer like an expert. At Ash's house, none of this was allowed without a parent. "What do you like in them?" Tilly asked while the mixer roared.

"In what?" said Ash.

"In the brownies!"

"Oh," Ash said. "Maybe nuts?" Unless Tilly was allergic.

Tilly opened the kitchen cabinet and said, "We have almonds. We also have coconut, chocolate chips, gummy bears, and crushed-up candy canes." She put them all on the kitchen table and said, "To be honest, my specialty is brownies with all of these things. I call them Everything Brownies."

Ash smiled. "All right, let's have those!" she said, and it sort of broke the ice. She scooped up the candies while Tilly mixed flour into the batter by hand. "My mom says you don't want to overmix the flour," Tilly said. "But I don't worry about adding in too much stuff. The more add-ins, the better, I think. It's like everything pizza, you know?"

"Or everything bagels," Ash pointed out.

"Yes!" said Tilly. "I love everything bagels!" So that was another thing they had in common.

Once the brownies went into the oven, they returned to the island. "Let's kick it up a little," Tilly said. "Are you good with some sequins?" There was no need to hunt for them—they were already in a heap on the rug.

"Sure," said Ash. Tilly glued them down in Terrapin Lake.

"And you know," said Tilly, "I was thinking that some sea turtles should live on the island. Like it shouldn't just be in the *shape* of a turtle."

"Totally!" said Ash. "Do you have any pipe cleaners?" She happened to be an expert in sculpting animals out of pipe cleaners, ever since she got a craft kit last Christmas.

"Right over there," Tilly said, pointing to a plastic bag stuffed under the couch. "When it comes to crafting, I have it all."

By the time the brownies were ready, the girls had embellished Sea Turtle Island with so many different art supplies that it was really more about the supplies than the turtles. It was shiny with sequins and sharp where the pipe cleaners poked out from the backs of the animals. And there were all kinds of animals now—keeping the turtles company—stuck in a slurry of wet paint.

Ash stood back and looked at the mess they had made. Usually she liked things to be neat and organized. Predictable. Correct. But there was something cool about this chaos—something that made her feel like she was free. Maybe this project was more than a Sea Turtle Island. Maybe it was something bigger and much, much better.

"I have an idea," she told Tilly. Or was it a wish?

"What if we give it a new name?" Ash almost didn't want to say it out loud. What if her idea was wrong?

But Tilly was on the same wavelength. She stood up and surveyed the island from above, then broke into a grin. She put on an announcer's voice and spoke to an imaginary audience, proclaiming, "Welcome to Everything Island!"

Chapter Thirteen

Ash had forgotten Gracie's soccer practice, or her ride home, until her dad texted to say he was on his way to pick her up. "So soon?" said Tilly.

"You can come to my house next time," Ash said. Suddenly that sounded like a good plan.

They weren't sure what to do with the island, though. "We'll need it at school, right?" said Tilly.

"I think so," Ash said. "But do you always take the bus? What if it gets crushed?"

"My bus is the worst!" said Tilly. "Maybe you should take the island home, and then you can just carry it to school."

"I'll be careful," Ash promised. Then her dad pulled into the driveway, and it was time to go. Ash carried the island gingerly down the stairs, wondering when Tilly's mom would come home.

"Tilly lives at a bakery?" Gracie said, craning her neck to see it from the back seat. "No fair!"

Ash didn't know how to describe the apartment, or their playdate, or whatever it was. It wasn't like any time she'd ever spent with Jane.

"Is that your island?" asked Gracie. "I love it!" Ash held it proudly, careful not to let the wet paint drip.

Her dad didn't weigh in until they got home and Ash left the island on the kitchen counter to dry. "What is that?" he asked. He was squinting, so his nose looked wrinkled, almost like he smelled something bad. Was it the paint? Ash wondered.

"It's Everything Island!" she exclaimed. "My project for Island Night."

Her dad walked around it, observing the island from every angle. "What's that yoke?" her dad asked, pointing at an orange blob. That was how Irish people said, "What's that thing?" His tone was light, but Irish words were never a good sign.

"A giraffe," Ash explained. "The island has every kind of animal, every color, every shape. Every geographical feature, too—we're still working on that." She smiled. She and Tilly had more ideas than they could fit on one island.

"That's part of the assignment?" her dad asked. Ash nodded. "When is it due?"

"At the end of the week," she said. "The next week is the fair. It's like a show, remember?"

Her dad let out a half sigh, half whistle. "Well, you still have some time to finish it, I guess. Wouldn't want anyone to see it quite yet, would you?"

Was it a metaphor to say that someone's mood was deflated? That was how Ash felt right now, like a bike tire that had just met a nail. Her mood, so joyful just moments ago, was leaking air.

Her dad offered some helpful suggestions. "If you need a new piece of posterboard, just let me know—I can run out and get it, no worries. And do you want to think about asking for some extra time to finish?"

There were kids who needed extra time for tests at school, but Ash had never been one of them. She certainly wasn't about to be one now.

Maybe he could feel the hurt coming off her like steam. "I'm only after trying to help, Aisling," her dad said. There was a hint of his Irish accent, so he was definitely upset.

Ash was upset, too. She picked up the island and raced to her room, her heart pounding. She wished she had said something, but what? Her dad could pretend he was trying to help, but she saw right through that. When he looked at her island, he didn't see the rush of imagination that had brought it into being. He thought only about her grade, and the GT program, and how she could get back in. Ash could fix the giraffe, but she couldn't fix her confidence, or this whole situation. Would her Island Project ever be good enough to get her back to Mr. Lopez? Would it ever be good enough for her parents? Whatever she was learning with this project, her father didn't understand.

Then there was a knock at her door. "I'm busy," Ash snapped. "I need a little space, okay?"

A soft voice said, "It's not Dad, Ash. It's me, Gracie."

Before Ash could even invite her in, Gracie was through the door. "I'm here to paint your nails," she said. She was carrying a bottle of neon-yellow nail polish, the same color as her soccer jersey. "Our first game is coming up, so we're all doing manicures in the team colors," she said. "We're also putting yellow streaks in our hair!"

"Well, I'm not on the team," Ash said glumly.

"Yeah, I know that, Ash," said Gracie. "But you're our biggest fan, right?"

Ash just wanted to be left alone. But Gracie didn't mention anything about the island, at least not at first. She painted Ash's right hand, and the polish on two of the fingers got all gummed up, so Ash had to take it off. When Gracie tried again, she painted more of Ash's skin than the nails. Luckily, they had plenty of nail polish remover and cotton balls.

"I think your island is awesome," Gracie finally said. "Don't listen to Dad. It's just . . . extra. So he doesn't get it."

Ash looked at her nails. "Mom and Dad really want me to get back to Mr. Lopez," she said. "But is the Island Project even going to make a difference? How much can that one grade even matter? I don't want to change the island now." When she said it out loud, she knew that it was true.

Gracie applied an extra coat of yellow before she said something radical. "How much does Mr. Lopez even matter?" She rushed to finish before Ash could cut her off. "I just mean he's not the only good teacher. There's more to Quigley than Mr. Lopez."

Was that wishful thinking, or was she onto something? Ash couldn't decide.

"But junior high . . . ," she said miserably. "And college!"

Gracie frowned, dabbing at a thick drop of nail polish. "Are you seriously worried about *college*?" she asked. "That's, like, fourteenth grade! You sound like Dad. Or

Jane." She blew on Ash's fingers until Ash curled them up and moved them away. "Do you want my advice?" Gracie asked.

No, Ash thought. But it was coming anyway.

"Don't let them push you around," said Gracie.

Ash bristled. She didn't let people push her around! She hoped she was still a girl who was going places, a leader and all that. But for some reason she thought about the upcoming summer vacation, not so far away now. Would she go to robotics camp, like her mom wanted? Or did she dare to try something different?

Ash closed her eyes. "Thanks, Gracie," she said. "My nails look great!" Gracie took the hint and slipped away, leaving Ash alone in her room at last. Ash flopped down on her bed and stared at the pink walls that had looked the same since as long as she could remember. She couldn't wait to put that patch of blackboard paint in here, and maybe pack up the rest of her old toys. She couldn't wait to meet the new Ash. Junior high Ash, whoever she was.

The paint on the island was almost dry now. Ash

hated to admit it, but Gracie had a point. She couldn't let her dad get to her. What would Tilly think if Ash went and started all over, just because her dad didn't understand the project? Tilly could make her own brownies! So Ash was going to have to make a decision one way or another, and she was pretty sure she knew what it would be. It felt like she was at the beginning of something, but also at the end.

There was another ending Ash had to write before the weekend was over. Even though she'd promised Mrs. Shepard, Ash still hadn't written that apology letter to Mrs. Silver. What was she supposed to say? How had the principal put it, again? Ash sat at her desk with a pile of stationery and wrote on the top page: *Dear Mrs. Silver, I'm sorry I undermined your hard work.*

Ash wasn't sure what that meant, so she looked it up. To undermine, it turned out, was to destroy something in a sort of sneak attack. If you dug a tunnel under someone's fort, say, you'd be undermining it. Ash sighed. She hadn't meant to make any attack at all. She hadn't meant to embarrass Mrs. Silver or anyone else involved in the Quiz Bowl. Ash couldn't even imagine what it took to get the whole event organized every year. There were a lot of people and a lot of cookies. All Ash had wanted was to win.

Was it right to say the event was destroyed, though, she wondered? Was anyone really hurt? The Quiz Bowl had raised money, just as it was supposed to, and only a few people knew the real story of how Ash had won. Jane *felt* hurt, definitely, but there were plenty of disappointed kids, no matter what. That happened every year. Only one person could win.

It would be better, Ash thought, if more people could win. If one person winning didn't mean so many other people losing. What if there could be a winner in each category? One for science, one for geography, one for movies, and so on. That way, even Sammy Silver could win once in a while.

Back when they were little, Ash and Gracie had taken Irish dancing lessons, and Ash still remembered her parents' reaction when she brought a prize home after the end-of-year recital. Or at least she'd thought it was a prize until her parents set her straight. "A trophy for what?" her mom had said, laughing. "Just for showing up?" Ash didn't think her idea for the Quiz Bowl was quite like that, though. Different kids knew different things. Not many kids knew everything—not even Ash, actually. Could it hurt to give more kids a chance?

It was easier to write the letter after Ash added her suggestion to the apology. *I got caught up in winning the Quiz Bowl, and I went way too far*, Ash wrote. *I didn't mean to ruin it for anyone else, though. And I have an idea for making it better for more kids next year.* Ash would be in the audience next year, when Gracie was in fifth grade. And, okay, Gracie wasn't usually a big competitor in the Quiz Bowl. But why not? Gracie was smarter than people knew.

When Monday morning rolled around, Ash carried Everything Island to school with pride. She was sticking with it—her decision was made. "I see you've made some changes," Ms. Cooper said when she arrived. "You've come a long way since Friday!" There was a shelf in the back of the classroom for islands-in-progress, and

Ash put hers on the edge that was farthest away from Caden's desk. She happened to know he had a bottle of fruit punch in his desk, the kind that was bright red and super sticky, and she wasn't taking any chances.

By the time Tilly arrived with the kids from her bus, Morning Meeting was about to start. Ash smiled and waved, and Ellie caught her doing it. "Wait, you're friends now?" she said, leaning over Caden's desk to look at Ash.

"Wait till you see our island!" Ash replied.

Ms. Cooper started Morning Meeting with a couple of yoga poses and some announcements about the field trip to Funtown at the end of the week. The Word of the Day was *fortitude*, and no one had any clue that it meant "strength." Ash and Caden turned to each other and said, "Fail!" at the exact same time, laughing.

For language arts this morning, Ms. Cooper had the class pull their chairs into a few small circles for a discussion. Ellie motioned to Ash that she should join her circle, and Ms. Cooper asked, "So, who can tell Ash and Tilly about our graphic novel?"

Ash missed the explanation while she worried about

whether she was in the right place. Was this the top group? she wondered. Tilly was in it, so maybe. Or was there a top group at all? She looked to Ms. Cooper for confirmation, but she couldn't catch the teacher's eye.

It was up to Ellie to fill Ash in on what they were doing. "So we read *El Deafo* with Ms. Cooper a while ago," she explained. "And now we're identifying figures of speech in it, to wrap up the unit."

Tilly picked up Ellie's copy of the book. "Looks great!" she said. "I love graphic novels!" Which made sense, Ash thought, because Tilly loved art. But she hadn't been at Quigley yet back when they'd read it.

Ash had read *El Deafo* in her library's summer reading program last year. She'd liked it way better than *Animal Farm*, plus she was basically a pro with the figures of speech by now, so she'd probably have a lot to add to this discussion. Or at least that's what she thought until Charlie scooted over to share her book, saying, "We're supposed to keep an eye out for metaphors first."

Ash's heart sank. She was disgraced and exiled only to come right back to where she'd started?

"You know what metaphors are, right?" Charlie confirmed.

"Yeah," said Ash. Kind of.

Tilly nodded. "We studied them at my old school, too," she said.

So Ellie got the group going. They went through the book page by page, paying close attention to the language and art now that they all knew what happened in the story.

"See this empty speech bubble?" Ellie said. "That could be a metaphor, right? For not hearing anything?" The book's main character was deaf, and the words in the speech bubbles disappeared when she had trouble with her hearing aids.

Good point, Ash thought. The other kids were nodding. She was embarrassed that she didn't have anything to contribute. If this was the highest reading group, she might not be at the top. Was she even gifted anymore? She shrank into her seat as people kept adding to their list.

Then Tilly, of all people, had something to say. "Do

you think it's a metaphor that all the characters are rab-bits?" she asked the others. "I mean, the book is about hearing—or not hearing—and rabbits have huge ears."

Ash looked at Tilly. How did she figure that out so fast? She hadn't even read the book! Ash wished she had picked up on that herself.

But no one else seemed upset that they'd missed this metaphor—Ellie even said, "Nice! I love that."

Ash had to agree. And actually, she realized, it was eas-ier to spot the metaphors when there were pictures along with the words. She suddenly had a hopeful thought, like a flashlight in a dark room. What if she could catch up on metaphors—at last—with the help of some illustra-tions? Would that be cheating, somehow? Or would it be finding a different way to figure them out?

Suddenly she felt like Caden, trying to conquer the triangles. But maybe it was okay. If they were all going to the same place, did she always have to get there first?

Chapter Fourteen

With just a few days till the islands were due, Ms. Cooper gave her students a lot of class time to fine-tune their work. Some kids were almost finished, but Ash and Tilly were still working hard because they'd started late. They took over a corner of the class-room and spread their supplies all over the place, so that it almost looked like Tilly's rug at home. Because the girls had so much space, Caden and his partner, Will, were wedged into a spot by the windows, but Ash tried not to feel bad about it. How many times had Caden's things overflowed onto her desk?

Ash read off the assignment sheet to make sure they had all the necessary elements. "A river, a mountain, a desert, a lake . . . ," she listed. "We've got them all. Oh—a compass rose?" That was the picture that told people which way was north on the map. They couldn't forget that!

"I'm on it," said Tilly. She sketched an elaborate rose in a corner of their model, to be painted later. Tilly was the lead artist on this island, for sure. Her sketches were better than most people's final pictures.

Every fifth grader had to answer questions about the location and economy of their island. So where *was* Everything Island? Ash and Tilly decided it was in the middle of the Pacific Ocean, halfway between the equator and the South Pole. The climate? Naturally, it had all four seasons, allowing every kind of storm from blizzards to hurricanes. "How do people earn a living?" Ash asked.

"They do a little bit of everything!" Tilly said. The girls came up with some examples, just in case. On their island, some people were plumbers, some were pilots, some were peanut farmers.

Once they had answered all the questions, the island was complete. Anyone who made it that far would get an A. But once they reached the finish line, Ash and

Tilly kept on going. *Working with Tilly is like playing pretend*, Ash thought. Like way back when she was little. They had so many ideas that the girls kept interrupting each other, and with each idea the island grew more crowded. It wasn't like working with Jane, where one person was the boss. It was more like working on a team.

Tilly designed a coin that you could use to buy anything—or everything—on the island. It had a sea turtle on it, in honor of where they'd started, but it came in every color of the rainbow. "We can give them out at Island Night!" she said.

"I'm just thinking about the Koala Café," Ash said. That was one of the buildings they'd put on the island—a restaurant, of course. "What if we make a menu for it? Then people can use their coins to buy something delicious."

"I love it!" Tilly exclaimed. "What kind of food should we have?"

"Well . . . every kind of food, don't you think?" Ash said. "An everything restaurant on Everything Island!"

It didn't take long to decide that the Koala Café should offer pancakes, burritos, smoothies, sushi, and chocolate pudding.

They had just started to make up some words in the island's language when Caden ventured into their space. He wasn't in mayhem mode—he was just admiring their project.

"Everything Island is awesome," he said sincerely.

"Thanks, Caden," said Tilly, who finally knew everyone in the class. "Would you like to see the menu from the Koala Café?"

"Your island has a restaurant?" Caden said in disbelief. "Oh, man, you're way ahead of me and Will, as usual." He shook his head and looked at Ash. "That's why you go to Mr. Lopez, I guess."

"I guess," she echoed. It wasn't like she got special lessons in island making there. This was a different kind of being smart.

Caden rolled his eyes. "Come on," he moaned. "Look at yours, then look at mine." Fortnite Island was on a wrinkled piece of posterboard, with its lettering in a faint colored pencil that Ash could barely see. It had everything it was supposed to have, but it needed some help.

"You should outline the letters in black," Tilly said. "They'll be easier to read that way."

"If you put something heavy on top of it overnight, it might smooth out," Ash added.

"No, no," Caden said. "What Will and I need is something special. Like . . . how did you know to make a restaurant? What should we *do*?" It was as if he didn't trust himself to have a good idea.

Ash looked at Tilly. "How did we know what to do?" she asked. "It just . . . made sense."

Tilly nibbled on the end of a marker. "Yeah, Fortnite Island doesn't need a restaurant. It needs something that goes with *Fortnite*."

Caden thought that over. He just stood there, as still as Ash had ever seen him, until his eyes lit up. It was actually like someone had hit an on switch. "I know! It needs a video game!" he said. Ash couldn't imagine how he and Will would develop a whole game in a few days, but Caden seemed pretty excited.

Ms. Cooper propped Ellie's project, Ice Cream Island, on her desk for others to use as a model. "This is bright, clear, and successful," said Ms. Cooper. "Well done!" Then she roamed from group to group, answering questions and offering advice. When she came to Ash and Tilly, she said, "This, girls, is a glorious mess."

Ash's face fell. "It's a good thing, Ash!" said Ms. Cooper. "You're taking some risks here. Plus your enthusiasm is carrying over to the other students, inspiring them to do their best work, too. This is exactly what I love about having you in my class!" Everything she said sounded like it had an exclamation point.

It was weird to get praise for making a mess and for telling other kids what to do. Would that kind of success get Ash back into the GT room? She shoved that question to the back of her mind, squashing it down as far as it would go.

Ash still had flashes of that fearful feeling that she

was always supposed to know things, but there was another feeling, too. Maybe it was because the sky was blue, the playground was dry, and the sun felt almost warm. Maybe it was because the calendar in Ms. Cooper's room was down to only about six weeks till summer now, and many of those weeks were packed with activities for the fifth graders, from the field trip to Island Night to Step-Up Day and the Manners Banquet. Whatever it was, Ash felt lighter. Brighter. Part of the grade in a new way. She used to like being apart and above, but now she liked being in the middle of things, too. It was like pitching a game of kickball—so much better than being marooned in left field.

She did not feel in the middle of anything, though, on Friday. That was the day of the field trip to Funtown, and possibly the worst day Ash had ever had at Quigley Elementary.

By the time she got to school, her class was long gone, as the school buses had departed at dawn for a three-hour drive. No one saw her staying behind, so at least she didn't need to come up with some cover story, but she was supposed to spend the day alone in the school library, working on extra assignments. And what if she was spotted by a kid from another grade? Ash spread her papers between the stacks, hoping that no one came to search for a book.

She was stuck here, of course, because she had broken the rules of the Quiz Bowl. But when her phone vibrated in her pocket, Ash broke another rule—no devices during school—to see who had texted. It was Tilly, sneaking in a message on her own just-for-emergencies phone. Throughout the day, she kept Ash updated on the trip.

It was hard to see pictures of Tilly with Ellie and the other girls, glued to the side of a spinning ride or hurtling downward on the zero-gravity drop. Ash had looked forward to the fifth-grade field trip for as long as she could remember, and now she'd never know what it was like. But Tilly managed to shoot a video of their ride on the three-loop roller coaster, and it almost made Ash feel like she was there. **Miss u!** said Tilly's message. Ash missed Tilly, too.

Just when Ash was easing into the final stretch of this endless day, a familiar bald head popped up on the other side of the shelves.

"Ash McNulty? Is that you back there?" asked Mr. Lopez.

At least Ash didn't need to tell him why she wasn't on the field trip. He could put two and two together.

"I've been thinking of you," he said, walking around the bookshelf to find her sprawled out on the carpet with her work. "How are things going upstairs?"

He meant her regular classroom, Ms. Cooper's. And how *were* things going? It was hard to explain.

"Okay, I guess," Ash stumbled. "We're doing metaphors, if you can believe it. I will never escape!"

She laughed nervously. There was something else she needed to say. "Mr. Lopez . . . ," she started. "I'm really sorry. About . . . everything." Maybe he could fill in the rest?

Mr. Lopez nodded and stroked his chin. He looked like he was thinking hard. "Listen, kiddo," he said. "Let's just say I'm sorry, too."

Ash frowned. "What for?" she asked. He hadn't done anything wrong!

Mr. Lopez sounded nervous, too. "Just that this happened at all. We do some great work in my classroom, right? But it's not the be-all and end-all. There are bright kids in every corner of the school. No one outside my room should feel . . . less. I don't want that to be your takeaway, shall we say."

True, Ash thought. Only one kind of bright kid got to go to Mr. Lopez.

His tone was firmer than usual. "Your job is not to know everything already, Ash. Your job is to keep growing, a little bit every day. And you can do that in *any* classroom, as long as your teachers give you the challenges you need."

Ash smiled. "Ms. Cooper is challenging me, all right," she said. Ms. Cooper was giving Ash some hard work and making her do some hard things.

"You've got a great future ahead of you, Ash," Mr. Lopez said.

It was nice to hear that again, after Ash had messed

up so badly. She waited for him to say something about her coming back to his room, but he didn't mention it and she didn't bring it up. Also, there was something much more important she wanted to know! "Hey, how's your puppy?" she asked.

Ash managed to flee the library before the rest of the fifth grade returned, and then it was the weekend. The McNultys had planned carefully for this Saturday, as it was the day of Gracie's first soccer game, and Gracie insisted that the whole family needed to be there. "That's what people do," Gracie said. "Some parents even watch games that their own kids aren't in!"

When the family arrived at the Dome that afternoon, Gracie practically flew out of the car, her neon-yellow-streaked ponytail bouncing behind her. Game day was like Christmas morning for Gracie, but for Ash it was an excursion to a strange land.

She and her parents huddled together awkwardly while Gracie's team warmed up. Some of the other families set up special chairs on the bleachers, to give them back support and protect them from the cold metal, but Ash's family didn't have the right gear. The other families came with large bags full of extra water and snacks—Ash even spotted a first aid kit—while the McNultys just had a bag of potato chips. Or crisps, as her parents called them. These were a brand that her dad ordered direct from Ireland—cheese-and-onion flavored—and they were way better than any American chips. Ash wished the McNultys blended in a little better, but she was also glad to have chips instead of protein bars designed for peak performance.

Since the players came from towns all over the place, Ash's parents didn't know any of the other parents on Gracie's team. Some of them seemed to know Gracie, though. When the starting players' names were announced, one of the moms yelled, "Woo-hoo! Gracie McNulty!" while Ash and her parents clapped politely. Had the other families watched all the practices? Ash wondered. The last time Ash had been here, Gracie had trouble controlling the ball.

She'd come a long way since then, though, Ash had to admit. The Gracie in this game was nothing like the Gracie that Ash had seen at practice and more like the Gracie everyone feared in kickball. She was a ferocious defender, aggressive and fearless, and Ash heard a couple of girls on the opposing team say, "Watch out for number four!" Ash filled up with pride and something like relief.

Sometimes she worried about her sister, focusing on soccer instead of school, but at least she was learning to play the game. All her practice was paying off, and now the whole Dome could see Gracie's talent shining.

Suddenly Ash had an uncomfortable memory of that rewrite she'd skipped, the practice she didn't do. What if talent wasn't only something you *had*, but something you *did*? Ash blinked, recognizing a big idea when she saw one. Then the girls closed in on Gracie, trying to shut her down. Gracie wove expertly between them, and Ash yelled, "Way to go!"

Gracie scored two goals even though she was supposed to be playing defense, and her team won decisively, 4–2. "This deserves a celebration!" said Ash's mom, so of course they went straight to The Gate.

The family had all gathered at a corner table and started looking at the menus even though they didn't need to, when Gracie whispered something to Ash. "Don't look," she said. "But you'll never guess who's here."

It was Jane's mom again, as if she had never left. She was even sitting at the same place, though she seemed to be with a different friend. She hurried over as soon as she spotted the McNultys. Ash wanted to hide under the table. What had Jill heard about the Quiz Bowl? she wondered anxiously. She still didn't know.

To Ash's surprise, though, Jill wanted to talk about her dinner. "The poached salmon was just astonishing," she gushed to Ash's dad. "And the potato gratin was nothing short of sublime." She looked at her friend and smiled. "No one knows how to do potatoes like the Irish," she declared.

People in Ireland did like potatoes, Ash knew, and not just in crisps. Long ago, when the potato crops failed, a million Irish people had starved without them and another million fled the country.

Ash thought Jill was being nice. But as she was walking into the upstairs bathroom at home that night, Ash overheard her parents talking in their room. "It's outrageous, Clare," said her dad. "Offensive, really. As if that's all we're good for."

"We could create new recipes for the next ten years," Ash's mom agreed, "and Jill would only see what she wants to see. Her idea of what's Irish. Like every day is Saint Patrick's Day."

Ash squeezed out some toothpaste and looked in the mirror as she brushed her teeth. Her parents both loved and hated Saint Patrick's Day. It was always good for business at The Gate, but they were embarrassed by the leprechaun stories, the pot of gold at the end of the rainbow, and the customers drinking too much green beer. "It's a stereotype," her mom had explained to Ash and Gracie. "There's more to Irish culture than rowdy people going to parades one day each March."

Her parents were trying to show another side of

Ireland at the pub now. They were using local ingredients to cook food inspired by that other side of Ireland, the one that people didn't know. So why was Jill stuck on the same old stereotype? Ash wondered. She spit out her toothpaste and swished water around in her mouth. Her parents were trying to be one thing, but Jill could only see them the other way, as if she had already made up her mind who they were.

It's like she doesn't even know them, Ash thought. *And maybe she doesn't really know me, either.*

Chapter Fifteen

After school on Monday, Ash made a quick stop at home before returning to Quigley for Island Night. Where was that shirt her aunt had brought back from her trip to Hawaii? Ash found it crumpled in the back of a drawer, but it looked okay after she shook it out. The shirt was bright pink, with yellow flowers splashed all over and a palm tree embroidered on the pocket. It was perfect for Everything Island—and, even better, Gracie had a matching one! Ash packed up the extra one for Tilly and rushed back to school. She couldn't believe there was still a whole hour left until Island Night began! How could she ever wait that long?

Tilly had stayed after school to help Ms. Cooper set up, and right now they were hanging the final few islands from their class in the hallway. Farther down the hall, other fifth-grade teachers were doing the same. Slowly, the second floor of Quigley Elementary was transforming into something like a museum.

"Now, of course we can't hang up all of them," Ms. Cooper said. "Those of you who made models will need a different way to show them." Ash and Tilly pulled some desks out of their classroom and set them up in the hallway nook, beneath a skylight.

Tilly buttoned up her tropical shirt and said, "Selfie?" No one would care if they had their phones now, so she and Ash took tons of pictures, some where they looked sweet and some where they stuck their tongues out. Then they spread their project carefully across a desk as the hallway filled up with visitors.

Each student would be stationed near their island, ready to tell visiting parents all about their work. Any minute now, Ash thought, and she'd be showing everyone she knew around Everything Island! Until then, there was one more important piece of business to take care of.

Tilly went into their classroom and came back with a long white envelope that had their names on the back. "Are you ready?" she asked Ash dramatically. Their grade from Ms. Cooper was inside.

And, okay, Ash wasn't expecting a bad grade—she and Tilly had done everything the assignment had called for, plus much more. Still, she was relieved when Tilly opened the envelope and let out a low whistle. Ms. Cooper had given them an A plus, along with some written comments. "This project demonstrates an understanding of the concepts as well as an understanding of the way geography connects to culture. Ash and Tilly, you've learned all I hoped, and then some. Nice job letting curiosity and creativity guide you past all my expectations!"

"Yes!" said Tilly, turning to give Ash a high five. Ash tasted the familiar flavor of success, sweeter because she knew she'd been honest this time. Maybe her parents would stop nagging her at last?

Still, there was that worry in the back of Ash's mind. Was this grade going to land her back in Mr. Lopez's class? Did she even want that, at this point? No one had said how or when it would happen, though Ash imagined her parents had been asking. Returning to Mr. Lopez would mean getting back everything Ash had lost, but it would also mean losing everything she had gained. Like time in school with a new friend. Could Tilly come to Mr. Lopez, too?

Pretty soon, the upstairs hallway was crammed with fifth-grade families, and Ash could hardly hear herself think. The students were talking about their islands, and the parents were also talking about a thousand other things. After a long winter, they had a lot to catch up on, from softball sign-ups to summer plans.

Tilly wasn't taking any chances that someone might miss their island. As someone's dad passed the hallway nook, Tilly collared him. "Welcome to Everything Island," she said as if she were a tour guide. "We have a little bit of everything."

Ash pressed a couple of sea turtle coins into his hands, following Tilly's lead. The girls had painstakingly cut them out of cardstock one by one. "This currency will get you everything you could need or want here," she added.

"Like, for instance, some of our delicious local cuisine!" said Tilly. "Would you like to see a menu? We serve it all."

"Such a warm welcome!" said a mom nearby, playing along. "So . . . tell me about the terrain of this island. How far is it above sea level?"

Ash told her about the variety of landforms, while Tilly shared a few words from the island language. "*Ankthay uway* for visiting," she said. That meant "thank you" here on Everything Island. "Come again anytime."

It took a while for Ash's parents to find her, and when they arrived Ash's dad said, "I'm here to inquire about vacation rentals on Everything Island?" Ash was grateful that her parents were polite, even if they didn't love her project. Gracie took a bunch of coins and distributed them to people in the hallway.

Tilly actually shook hands with both of Ash's parents, and she could tell they liked that. "It's so nice to meet you," she said. Tilly spoke the way Ash and Gracie spoke when they were at The Gate. It was a whole new side of her, poised and smart. She was starting to get comfortable at Quigley.

"So, are your parents coming to Island Night, Tilly?" asked Ash's mom. "I look forward to meeting them." Ash was curious, too.

"My mom will come if she can," Tilly said. "My dad's not around."

"Oh?" said Ash's mom.

"He's in California," Tilly explained. "That's where we lived when I was little, before we left for Arizona, and then Florida. He's staying there, but my mom and I are . . . looking for a home base." Tilly sort of trailed off.

"Sounds like a lot of changes," Ash's mom said.

Tilly flashed her jagged smile, like she was relieved to leave it at that. "My mom is hoping we can settle down here." What would it be like to keep starting over? Ash wondered.

When Ms. Cooper swung by to check on the girls,

she encouraged them to take a break and see the other islands. "It's important to support the other fifth graders," she said. "And there's still some time until the awards." Ash and Tilly ventured out to see Ellie and Caden, whose posters were next to each other. For once, Caden respected Ellie's space. Or maybe he was too busy showing people how to play his video game? It was on a tablet that he passed around with pride.

They were about to turn back when Ash realized there was a group of students they'd missed at the end of the hall. They, too, had models instead of posters. It turned out they were the kids from the GT class, minus Sebastian.

Olivia's project was Endangered Species Island, divided into areas for the black rhino, the Amur leopard, and the hawksbill turtle. Olivia had sewn her own stuffed animals so everyone could see what the endangered species looked like.

Lane, of course, had taken the funny route. His island was dedicated to puns from *The Phantom Tollbooth*, one of his all-time favorite books. All the geographical features connected to characters from the story, and his whole island had a bright, bold style, like a comic book.

Ash couldn't even see Jane, since she was surrounded by people marveling at Moon Island. The island itself looked like a lunar landscape—that of Europa, which orbited Jupiter, Jane said—but all the rivers and mountains were named after other moons. Jane had even made scale models of these moons with marbles and covered them with paper the same color and texture as their atmospheres. Calculations showed the distances between these moons and their planets, plus their distance from the sun. The whole thing looked like something a college student might make. Or maybe a college professor.

"Whoa," said Tilly, shaking her head.

Ash could hear Jane explaining her work to admiring parents, saying things like, "Well, first I ran the numbers . . . ," and each word was a jet of cold water on Ash's joyful mood. She could have been at that table, too, impressing the adults. That island could have been her island. She hoped Tilly couldn't tell she was jealous.

As Ash struggled to say the right thing, the buzz in the hallway stopped and the principal's voice crackled on the PA system, reminding families to make their way to the gym. There would be a little ceremony for the fifth graders, since this was a milestone project, and there would also be some awards.

"So we just leave our island up here?" Tilly asked.

"I guess so," Ash said, shrugging. Somehow it felt like they were abandoning ship.

The scene in the gym was like the Quiz Bowl all over again, crowded and electric. Mrs. Shepard stood onstage with a microphone, and there were some small gifts on a table for her to distribute. Proud parents sat in the back of the gym—well, except for the ones who were standing up to take pictures—while the fifth graders sat in rows up front. Ash was happy with her grade, but she still had a familiar longing. In spite of everything, she wanted an award.

Up onstage, Mrs. Shepard tapped her mike. "To start, I'd like to welcome you all to the beginning of the end of the school year, as we celebrate our fifth graders and their many accomplishments at Quigley Elementary," she said. She scanned the crowd and happened to make eye contact with Ash. Her glance wasn't stern, but almost friendly. Almost like Ash had been forgiven.

The first gifts went to the teachers, for all their support of the fifth grade. Ash cheered for Ms. Cooper, and also for Mr. Lopez, who was wearing a tie with a lighthouse on it just for the occasion. He waved to the crowd and ducked his bald head modestly as he returned to his seat. Then there was a prize for use of technology—that went to Caden and Will, with their last-minute video game! And a prize for artistry, which somehow went to Lane.

Ash was second-guessing that choice when she heard her own name. "And now I'd like to give *two* prizes to a team from Ms. Cooper's class," said Mrs. Shepard. "A dynamic duo, Ash McNulty and Tilly Belvedere. These two are our winners for both creativity and teamwork. The theme of their island is, well, everything. And once they visualized its geography, they developed a culture and an economy for it, too. They had a big idea and they ran with it, together."

All the people clapped as Ash and Tilly went to the stage to collect small packages tied with bright blue ribbon. Ash's smile was so big that her face started to hurt. She was right back where she wanted to be, and it seemed right for Tilly to be at her side. After all, she'd almost won the Quiz Bowl.

Has she ever been a GT kid? Ash wondered. Well, no, she realized. Tilly hadn't lived anywhere long enough to take the test and get settled. A kid like that would never get to try.

When it was time for the grand prize, Ash was actually on the edge of her seat. Could this one also be theirs? She was hopeful until Mrs. Shepard described the winning island in detail, from its advanced mathematics to its imaginative design. "In Moon Island, we see not just an understanding of geography but a deep interest in science. As if this project is the springboard for another, larger project—a lifetime of learning."

The principal picked up the biggest gift, adding, "Jane Chapman-Haynes, congratulations."

Of course. Ash sighed. She'd never take the grand prize now, unless she cheated again. How had she even imagined it could be hers? She wasn't gifted, so she could go only so far. Ash was so focused on her own hurt feelings that it took a moment to realize Tilly was sniffling.

Mrs. Shepard wished everyone a lovely evening. People were getting up now, starting to leave for the night, but Tilly was glued to her seat. "It's not fair, Ash," Tilly whispered, blinking fast. "I think she got a prize because she always gets a prize. And I don't think she made that island all by herself."

Jane's island was awesome, but Tilly was right. Ash *knew* she was right.

Jill probably did help Jane. And the GT kids really did get praise they didn't earn—Ash knew that first-hand. After all, she remembered those weeks she'd been sliding by on her good reputation. It was kind of like what her parents had said about being Irish. People had made up their minds about who the GT kids were: winners. And so they won.

Now Ash was more angry than envious. Because was Jane's island *actually* better? Who could even decide? There were things you could measure, like answers on a math test or at a Quiz Bowl. Like Tilly had said, a robot could memorize those answers and spit them right back out.

But there weren't any right or wrong islands. A lot of them were good, in fact. Most of them had met the requirements, and many had gone above and beyond. So how could anyone pick a winner?

Tilly swiped a hand over her eyes to dry them. She took a sharp breath and tilted her chin defiantly. "It's fine, though. I'm fine. It is what it is." She had seen this all before, at other schools in other places. From the outside, she could see some things more clearly.

The stage curtain had come down, and the last families were leaving the gym. Nothing was going to change now.

It wasn't fair, but maybe it *was* fine, Ash thought. It was another big idea, and it almost took her breath away. She had taken a big risk to build the island of her dreams, but Ash had found a different kind of learning there, where knowing the answers wasn't what made you smart. It was the asking of the questions.

So, she got the best grade possible. She got two prizes out of this project, plus a new friend. Did she truly need more? Did she need to be "best" to be good? Maybe the label, or the prize, was not the point.

When Ash was really honest about it, she knew she didn't even care about the GT room anymore. She was looking toward summer now, toward junior high after that, and she wasn't going to let anyone push her around.

Chapter Sixteen

As a person who usually walked to school, Ash loved the chance to ride on a school bus. Other kids complained about feeling sick in the back row or the bus drivers yelling too much, but Ash loved the feel of the smooth seats—you had to hang on not to slip—and the sound of the fifth grade singing at the top of their lungs.

This was a big day for Ms. Cooper's class. Before they boarded the bus, Ms. Cooper had made groups for the Manners Banquet, which was on the last day of school. Ash and Tilly had been grouped with Caden and Ellie! Okay, Caden was going to have to do a lot of practice for the banquet, where the fifth graders wore their best clothes and ate food that required cutting with a knife and fork. But they would be all together, like at a restaurant almost! It was hard, now, to remember that Tilly was still new, or that Caden used to be just a pest. Both of them were growing on Ash, for sure. Maybe they could all get together to practice their manners at The Gate.

Now they were going for Step-Up Day at the junior high, which was another way of saying that they were going for a tour. They would meet some teachers, but they wouldn't actually have classes. The idea seemed to be for fifth graders to learn where the classrooms were, and maybe the bathrooms.

When the bus shuddered to a stop at the junior high's front door, Ash peered out the window. The first thing she saw was a bike rack full of adult-size bikes. No one here had training wheels, like the little kids at Quigley. This year's sixth graders were out of the building today, so there would be space for the new crop in their classrooms, but Ash spotted some older kids as her class trooped through the school's lobby. They had to be eighth graders, she thought. They almost looked like grown-ups. And did one of the boys have a mustache? Maybe it was a trick of the light. Ash and Tilly looked at each other in disbelief.

The junior high didn't gleam, like Quigley. It was in an old building without many windows, and Ash had heard that the floor in one of the classrooms sloped so sharply you could roll a ball downhill. She liked the feeling of the place immediately, though, with its worn floors and dented lockers. The teachers were all smiling, and the school felt cozy. Like Ash would be at home here.

Ms. Cooper turned her class over to a sixth-grade teacher, who led them down the hallway and explained what they were seeing. The sixth grade had different teachers for every subject, so they switched rooms for each class, and all those rooms were in one hallway. They wouldn't mix much with the older kids until they got to after-school activities.

There were a lot of those, the teacher went on, as a lot of learning happened outside of class. Kids could sing in a choir. They could play in a jazz band. They could start an a cappella group of their own. They could play any one of, like, nine sports—and they'd get to compete against other junior highs, all over the place, not just against one another.

Tilly was dazzled by the art room, while Ellie wanted to hear more about the school play. "There are two every year?" she asked in disbelief. There was a school newspaper and a yearbook, an environmental club, and a civil rights team. Could one person do every activity? Ash wondered. How would she ever choose?

There were plenty of familiar faces around the school, older siblings of kids that Ash knew, plus the sons and daughters of some servers from The Gate. But the last people she expected to see here were Mrs. Silver and Jane's mom. When they passed the principal's office, Ash spotted them in there, having a heated discussion with someone in a suit.

Sammy Silver turned pale and pretended not to notice. Junior high promised greater freedom for most of the fifth grade, but Sammy would never be free. Maybe his mom was here trying to get him into the GT class already. Ash noticed her tour guide hadn't mentioned the Talent Development program. But why would she? It applied to only a few people.

The whole fifth grade lined up in the auditorium to take ID pictures and register for classes, which really just meant checking off two boxes: your level of math and whether you planned to take French or Spanish. And then it was time to return for lunch at Quigley. Ash felt a pang of disappointment, then another pang of antic-ipation. Next year, she'd be here every day. Maybe she'd join the track team or sing in the choir. She would grow and stretch here. She couldn't wait to spread her wings.

Too soon, the whole fifth grade was crammed into the narrow lobby, waiting for the bus to bring them back to Quigley. But the bus was delayed because of rain, and another round of singing started. Ash got pushed to the back of the crowd and found herself right at the end of the lobby, where it opened into the school's first-floor hallway. Before she knew it, Ash was pinned against the trophy case.

And what a trophy case it was! While Quigley just displayed the honor roll by the office—and Ash tried never to look at it now—the junior high had a collection of treasures. There were silver cups and golden statuettes, prizes for everything from band to lacrosse, dating back for decades. There was a sparkling mask, for someone who'd played the lead in a show in 1998. There was a line of framed certificates for kids who'd won writing contests and a giant basketball that honored last year's championship team.

Ash could see her reflection in the glass, wide-eyed in awe. She thought back to that letter she'd written to Mrs. Silver, about giving prizes for different categories at the Quiz Bowl. This, Ash thought, was what she had in mind. In junior high, there would be many different ways to stand out. A kid could fail a class, even, but still find a way to be a star. No one would be the winner overall.

Ash was thinking that over when she saw another face reflected in the glass, gazing at these riches. It was Jane's. "Hi, Ash," she said quietly.

This was awkward, but right now Ash was full of goodwill toward all. Why not be nice to Jane, at last?

"What do you think?" Ash said. "What are you going to sign up for? There are so many choices!"

Jane shrugged. "I don't know. I haven't really thought about it yet. Jazz band, maybe? Or robotics club?"

Uh-oh, Ash thought. They were venturing into dangerous territory. Luckily, Jane changed the subject.

"So did you hear what happened?" she asked.

"With what?" said Ash.

"With the GT program. They're changing it at the junior high." Jane shook her head sadly. "We won't have our own class anymore, once we get here. My mom's trying to fight it, but we're going to be mixed in with everybody else."

"Oh," Ash said. "That's too bad." When the crowd started moving slowly toward the front door, she made a quick escape from her old friend. Everybody else, Ash knew, meant kids like her. No one special. Except now she knew other ways to be special, and Jane still had to learn.

Ash daydreamed through most of the afternoon. Could she audition for a play? she wondered. What did the environmental club even do? Did the junior high have a math team? She was still weighing her options when she arrived home after school. Her mom was in the kitchen, testing a new salad that included seaweed.

"Will you give it a taste?" Ash's mom asked.

Ash scrunched up her face. "No, thank you," she said as if she were at a Manners Banquet. "I don't . . . care for any seaweed." It was probably local, probably organic and sustainably harvested. Maine, like Ireland, had a coastline full of it. But Ash thought her parents were going one step too far in challenging stereotypes. No one wanted a seaweed salad, even if it was Irish green.

"Oh, your paperwork arrived," her mom said, tossing the salad with tongs. "It's on the table in the hallway."

When Ash tore open the envelope, she found her camp registration. The people in charge needed some information about her, like her height and weight. She'd be assigned her own personal flotation device, her own paddle, and even her own boat at kayak camp. Quickly, Ash texted Tilly. **Did you get your camp**

packet? The two girls were going together, and that way Tilly's mom wouldn't need to worry about child care all summer.

Ash could see the little dots indicating that Tilly was writing back. While she waited, she wandered back into the kitchen, where her mom was making a list. "Are you sure about this camp?" her mom said, not meeting her eyes. "I mean, robotics camp is really an opportunity. It's at a college, remember? A good place for a smart girl like you."

Ash made another face. She couldn't help it.

"I'm sure, Mom," she said. "Because kayak camp is going to be so much fun! And I'm not just a smart kid, you know? I'm an everything kid."

A Note to Readers

Not that long ago, my kids went to a school that looked just like Quigley, and it had a short-lived GT program like the one in this book, led by some incredibly dedicated teachers. This story is not about any of the real people from that school, whether kids or grown-ups, but it's rooted in some thinking I did at the time.

Somehow, back then, I found myself on a committee that met to discuss what the GT program should or could look like. There were important educational questions about how best to serve gifted-and-talented students, but I became more interested in the impact of calling kids gifted at all. Turns out that when some kids are elevated above others in school, a lot can potentially go wrong.

Sometimes a "gifted" label can actually make it more difficult for a child to handle challenges. Research shows that many gifted kids see intelligence as something hardwired, not as something they need to strive for. They dread losing their status as smart, so they avoid admitting when they don't understand things. And when it comes time for them to think creatively, they can be paralyzed with the fear of making a mistake—the very opposite of the growth mindset that schools try to foster.

It may seem like a nice problem to have, but this special status can come with a crushing pressure no one intends, which takes hold early and persists until the "right" college acceptances roll in a decade later. But such sky-high expectations don't acknowledge or nurture the messy, inconsistent process of growing up.

I hope readers will consider how labels—even good ones—can limit and define them. No one's identity should be built on being better than everybody else. It's also critically important to consider who is and is not eligible to be labeled gifted in the first place.

Way back when, people also thought I was a gifted child. I remember the golden feeling of being special, singled out, admired by adults. I also distinctly remember when my classmate Billy Goldman caught up with me. I was a different person then: second-rate and completely lost.

Now I know that was the moment when I started to smarten up.

Thank-Yous

Thanks to Helen Bernstein and Kristin Earhart, who were enthusiastic from day one.

Thanks to Nancy Gallt, who made me write an outline, and Liz Szabla, who pried the first three chapters out of my hands.

Thanks to Foyinsi Adegbonmire for such deft and thoughtful edits.

Thanks to Ramona Kaulitzki for the stunning cover.

Thanks to the whole Feiwel and Friends team for taking on this story and caring for it every step of the way.

Thanks to Charlotte Agell, Andrew Kosak, and Pete Stevens for weighing in so wisely.

Thanks to Josie Cameron and Cindy Lord for encouragement and morning glory muffins.

Thanks to Suzanne Collins for a kindness from out of the blue.

Thanks to my adopted hometown, Brunswick, for teaching me what public school can be.

Thanks to Sarah Chingos, Kate Kalajainen, Cindy Patterson, Heather Perkinson, Beth Pols, Jen Taback (and Tony T.) for walking so many miles by my side.

Thanks to John F. Egan, first-generation American and first-rate dad.

Thanks to the rock-solid Egan women, Maura and Liz, for a lifetime of reading, writing, laughter, and inspiration.

Thanks to Jonathan, Maddie, and Nate for all the rest. For everything, really, with love.

About the Author

Kate Egan's gifts and talents all involve words. She is the author of a picture book, *Kate and Nate Are Running Late!*, and a chapter book series, The Magic Shop, both published by Feiwel and Friends. Her work has been named to many state reading lists, selected by the Junior Library Guild, and recognized as "Best of the Year" by Amazon. She is also a freelance editor, a prolific ghostwriter, and an occasional book reviewer. Kate lives with her family on the coast of Maine.

Thank you for reading this Feiwel & Friends book.

The friends who made

possible are:

JEAN FEIWEL, *Publisher*

LIZ SZABLA, *Associate Publisher*

RICH DEAS, *Senior Creative Director*

HOLLY WEST, *Senior Editor*

ANNA ROBERTO, *Senior Editor*

KAT BRZOZOWSKI, *Senior Editor*

DAWN RYAN, *Executive Managing Editor*

CELESTE CASS, *Production Manager*

EMILY SETTLE, *Associate Editor*

ERIN SIU, *Associate Editor*

FOYINSI ADEGBONMIRE, *Associate Editor*

RACHEL DIEBEL, *Assistant Editor*

MALLORY GRIGG, *Senior Art Director*

HELEN SEACHRIST, *Senior Production Editor*

Follow us on Facebook or visit us online at mackids.com.

Our books are friends for life.